Praise for T

"...thigh-clenchingly HAWT!!!"
— Francesca, *Under the Covers Book Blog*

"Great characters, great story and steaming hot scenes fill the pages of this erotic Sci-Fi romance."
— *Bitten by Paranormal Reviews*

"There [sic] is not one moment of this book that doesn't make you sweat and beg for more."
— *Beth's Wild and Crazy Book Reviews*

"Ann Mayburn paints a stunning picture of the perfect world gone wrong."
— *Sensual Reads*

"...red-hot futuristic BDSM tale, which will keep you squirming in your seat furiously..."
— Victoria, *TwoLips Reviews*

"Ann Mayburn is quickly becoming one of my favorite authors and *The Breaker's Concubine* is part of the reason why."
— Mrs. C, *BlackRaven's Reviews*

LooseId®

ISBN 13: 978-1-61118-822-6
THE BREAKER'S CONCUBINE
Copyright © September 2012 by Ann Mayburn
Originally released in e-book format in October 2011

Cover Art by Anne Cain
Cover Layout and Design by April Martinez

All rights reserved. Except for use of brief quotations in any review or critical article, the reproduction or utilization of this work in whole or in part in any form by any electronic, mechanical or other means, now known or hereafter invented, including xerography, photo-copying and recording, or in any information storage or retrieval is forbidden without the prior written permission of Loose Id LLC, PO Box 809, San Francisco CA 94104-0809. http://www.loose-id.com

DISCLAIMER: Many of the acts described in our BDSM/fetish titles can be dangerous. Please do not try any new sexual practice, whether it be fire, rope, or whip play, without the guidance of an experienced practitioner. Neither Loose Id nor its authors will be responsible for any loss, harm, injury or death resulting from use of the information contained in any of its titles.

This book is an original publication of Loose Id. Each individual story herein was previously published in e-book format only by Loose Id and is a work of fiction. Any similarity to actual persons, events or existing locations is entirely coincidental.

Printed in the U.S.A. by
Lightning Source, Inc.
1246 Heil Quaker Blvd
La Vergne TN 37086
www.lightningsource.com

THE BREAKER'S CONCUBINE

Ann Mayburn

Chapter One

Prince Devnar Haylen shifted in his gravity boots as his anticipation increased with every beat of his heart. The Kyrimian ship had failed in its attempt to outrun theirs, and now it was time to see their prize. They waited in the air lock as their lasers cut out a hole in the side of the deep-space freighter and secured an entrance.

"No response from the freighter on our instructions to surrender. It looks like they're going to fight," Volun, his best friend and second in command, said through the communicator in Devnar's helmet. Back inside the ship, Volun kept watch for any approaching vessels and constantly scanned the captured freighter held in place by their magnetic tractor beam.

Unease twisted through Devnar's gut as they prepared to board. Not much was known about the Kyrimians; they kept their planet carefully isolated from the rest of the galaxy. According to the history books, something had happened thousands of years ago that partially destroyed Kyrimia. From that point on, the Kyrimians had adopted a strict nobody-on, nobody-off policy, and information about the planet and its people trickled to a halt. They didn't even allow foreign ships to enter their atmosphere. Instead they did all their trading from a base on one of their moons, and they handled all shipping themselves.

The largest source of the rare crystal zanthin for twenty light years, Kyrimia was guarded by a defense system even the most foolhardy raiders avoided. Zanthin was the fuel that enabled ships to travel at light speed, and it was extremely rare.

Devnar knew one thing about Kyrimia: it was the richest planet in the galaxy and well-known for sparing no expense on the items it imported. Whether the ship was returning from a shipping expedition or on its way to pick some cargo up, the freighter was a rare prize.

"You sure this is the ship your informant told you about?" Devnar asked Volun on a private communication link.

"Yeah, this is the one. Same galactic registry code and everything. My informant said they might put up a small struggle, but that it was mostly mercenaries and a few Kyrimians. The mercs should give up quick enough when they realize they're being boarded by a Jensian raiding party, and I don't think the Kyrimians will be a problem. Besides, our intelligence shows that this ship is loaded with zanthin." Two beeps sounded in Devnar's helmet as Volun switched back to the public channel. "Hold tight; the scan is almost done."

Anxiety and nerves had him repeatedly checking his weapons. With the blessings of the Goddess, there would be enough zanthin here to replenish the coffers at his home on Jensia and keep the rebel slavers on his planet at bay. It seemed like each year more men were lured by promises of women, however unwillingly detained, to join the rebels that held the southern portion of his planet. Only one in every twenty births on Jensia was a woman, a fact that led to great competition for their favors. The rebels in the south treated their women like slaves, trading and breeding them like cattle.

A low, metallic whine vibrated through the floor as the cutting was finished and their ships connected. On the other side of the small portal window, he could only see darkness as the wall fell away to reveal the inside of the freighter.

"Do we know anything about their personal weapons system?" Devnar asked as he shifted and tried to detect any movement on the other side of the door.

"Negative." Volun hesitated, and Devnar could see him in his mind. Right now Volun would be tapping his fingernails together like he always did when he was nervous or thinking. "This particular freighter was well outside of the safe shipping zones and seemed to be heading to a deserted section of this galaxy."

"What do you think they're hauling?" Ikel's voice sounded through the communication link in Devnar's helmet.

Shrugging, Devnar rolled his shoulders and rechecked his weapon. "Hopefully the information we received is correct, and it's loaded with zanthin. That's about the only thing that comes off that polluted hunk of rock they call a planet."

"Maybe some of their women will be on board," Volun said in a hopeful voice. "I heard they're absolutely perfect in every way and eager to please."

Devnar growled deep in his throat. "No prisoners. You want to be a slaver, join the rebels. Then you can steal all the women you want and keep them chained up like animals. Whip them until they scream every time a man enters a room."

Anger crept into Volun's voice. "I would never betray you, Prince."

Silence except for the hissing of his air purifier filled the holding bay as they waited for the scan to be completed. Ten years ago, Devnar's younger sister had been kidnapped by the rebels. When they finally rescued her, she had been beaten within an inch of her life and raped repeatedly. She had been unwillingly bonded by a dozen different males. He'd taken great satisfaction in hunting down every one of them and ending their lives. It was easily done; once a Jensian male had bonded to a female, they could find each other anywhere in the world. With his sister at his side, there had been no place they could hide where she couldn't find them.

Sucking in a breath through his nose, Devnar tried to rein in his temper. They had a job to do, and he wasn't going to be any good to his men if he let the past haunt him. "I know. Forgive me for my anger."

Volun's tone grew teasing, and Devnar grinned in spite of himself. "Forgiven, forgotten, and gone. A man can't help but wish for a mate. Hell, I'd even bond her with you if I had to. And I know how loudly you snore and how much your breath stinks after a night of drinking."

His men laughed over the communication link. Devnar smiled behind his visor. Because of the small amount of women on Jensia, polygamy was the norm. Devnar's mother had bonded with four men, so he had grown up with four fathers. His sire was the current king. He hadn't felt the primal urge to bond any of the available females, but he and Volun had shared a willing woman or two.

"You just like the way I taste," Devnar teased, and the other men roared with laughter. The erotic memory of Volun licking his spilled seed from between a woman's thighs flashed through his mind. Blood rushed to his cock in response, and he shifted as it swelled beneath his armor. Maybe after the raid, he and Volun could celebrate together.

Truth be told, Volun's seed was just as sweet. Evolution had shaped the males of their species into being able to detect another healthy male—possible mate—by their scent and the taste of their seed. A compatible male who would be a strong asset to his female would taste like life and passion. Each man's taste was unique, a complex blend of chemicals and hormones that his brain translated into aroma and flavor. Sampling another man's seed was a highly erotic and pleasurable experience, heightened only when it was mixed with a female's cream. Then it became an explosive combination that drove the males into a mating rut.

Volun chuckled, and the stats from the scanner ran across Devnar's visor plate. The beep of a private communication link sounded before Volun said, "Well, my prince, I'm glad I'm not the only one whose cock is excited." His tone changed from teasing to hard as he broadcast to all the men, "Slight movement down the corridor to the left. Only looks like one or two people. Could be personal guards coming to negotiate. Initiating battle protocol."

The purified air from Devnar's helmet tasted faintly of the chemicals used to speed up his metabolism and dull any pain. The other men around him grew still, all their instincts honed to the killing edge. Despite the fact that he only breathed air supplied by his armor, Devnar's nostrils flared as he instinctively tried to take in the scent of the captured ship.

Senses now heightened for battle took in the world around him. Muscles bred and hardened for war tightened with excitement. To capture a ship full of zanthin would go a long way toward securing his spot as the next ruler of Jensia, and buy them the supplies they needed to fight the rebels from the southern hemisphere of their planet.

"Eyes ahead," Devnar responded on the global link. Taking the lead, he switched his view to infrared. Behind him, six men followed him into the dark hallway. Cursing softly, he noted the walls of the ship were specially coated to conceal any heat signatures. The apprehension in his gut twisted again, and he gestured for his men to flank out behind him. Why would a small freighter need shielded walls?

He glanced behind him and pointed to the two older men with him. "Wilim and Montro, I want you guarding our backs in case we need to make a quick escape." Somewhere in the Kyrimian ship, a door opened and changed the pressure in the corridor. "This doesn't feel right."

The two men nodded at him and crouched next to the air lock with their weapons pointed down the hall.

A beeping sound in his helmet alerted him to the failure of his filtration system. Trying to find the source of the problem, he heard reports from his men of their own systems failing. It was too big of a coincidence. A trace of fear wormed into his belly. Why only sabotage their breathing systems? He took a deep breath, scenting the air on the back of his sensitive palate. With the hormones and chemicals of battle lust running through his blood, he could taste the musky hormones of his men and a faint hint of female. That feminine musk immediately captured his attention on every level and began to revert his thought process down to its primitive mating state.

Moving slowly, Devnar crept forward, drawn by that hint of female desire even as he struggled to resist its lure. The fragrance tickled his nose and went right to the root of his cock in a pounding rush of blood. Lust clouded his thoughts and turned his mind from warrior to predator. He had enough time to say, "My suit's been tampered with," before all conscious thought faded and he became a creature of need and instinct.

Dimly he was aware of someone shouting into his communication link for him to respond, but that didn't alarm him as it should have. Next to him, four of his men followed him down the hallway, all but running to chase the scent. There was a woman ahead, and as an unmated male of the warrior breed, he was helpless against his urges.

Weapon totally forgotten at his side, he stopped before a sealed door. Even though he knew it was impossible, he could almost see the scent trickling from the minute gaps around the seals.

"What do you mean your suit's been tampered with? Prince?" Volun's voice squawked through his headgear. "I'm detecting movement in your area. A lot of it. Get out of there!"

Instead of responding, Devnar snarled at one of his men as he caressed the brushed metal of the closed door. The female inside was his, and he would fight anyone to get to her.

"Prince!" Volun screamed into his ear now. "Get out! Get your men out! It's a trap!"

The words should have meant something to Devnar, but they did nothing to detract him.

A pair of hands grabbed his shoulders and tried to pull him away, but Devnar turned and hit Wilim hard enough to throw him against the wall. Montro hauled the man to his feet and avoided a punch Devnar threw. The older men backed away, and Devnar gave them a warning snarl before turning back to the door.

"What the hell's going on?" Volun yelled through the helmet.

"They're using the scent of a female in heat," Wilim responded in a rush. "I tried to get the prince, but he's in a mating rut. If he were alone, we might be able to subdue him, but with the other men in rut as well, we'll be torn apart if we try to take them away from what they think is a breeding female."

"Balls," Volun said. "Get back on the ship."

"But the prince—"

"I said get back on the ship! That's an order!"

The men arguing on his headset annoyed Devnar, and he flicked off the communication link. The scent of a female in need swamped the air; his erection throbbed in response. His body demanded release, so he took off his armor, fingers fumbling with the straps and clamps as, behind him, the sound of metal hitting the floor filled the corridor. He tossed his weapon to the side and stretched with a moan. The feeling of his hair hitting his shoulders was like a caress to his aroused body.

Everything that touched his sensitive skin hurt. He had to be ready to present himself for the female's inspection. The air cleared for a moment as movement farther down the corridor pushed it away. It gave him enough time to scream in fury. Drugs. Someone knew their weakness and was pumping the air full of synthetic hormones to trigger their mating urges.

Blinding lights filled the corridor, and he pressed his palms to his sensitive eyes. The small ship rocked as their raiding vessel detached. He sent a silent prayer to his Goddess that Volun would get away. If he could manage to escape, it wouldn't take him long to rescue them. They wouldn't be taken to Kyrimia itself, probably to one of the planet's moon stations.

"Filthy raiders." A male voice pierced Devnar's ears. His lips pulled back in a silent snarl. He struggled to regain himself, to battle the effects of the aphrodisiac. Trying to tell his aroused body there was no worthy female to fight over was useless.

A woman's voice, cold and cruel, sounded from nearby. She spoke in a low tone, and he was unable to make out most of her words, but one did come through loud and clear. *Prince.* They knew who he was. Gritting his teeth, he flexed his hands and tried to judge the distance between himself and his weapons.

His cock was still rock hard, but his mind rejected the woman as a mate, and it helped him regain his self-control. Something about her psychic and physical smell repulsed him as much as the synthetic one aroused. Blinking against the lights, he curled his hands into fists and tried to assess the situation. His four remaining men were all naked, with their armor discarded next to his farther down the hall. Judging by their dilated pupils and hard cocks, they were as affected by the hormones as he was.

Every bit as beautiful and perfect as Volun had hoped, a tall woman with dark black skin covered in a shimmering canary yellow gown smirked at him. The cruelty in her gaze offset any physical beauty. Her scent reminded him of spoiled meat. Behind her stood at least three dozen guards, all armed to the teeth. Shit, Volun was right. Someone set them up. Guilt and fury battled within him as he tried to think of a way to save his men.

"What's our ransom price?" he spat out and lifted his chin. If she knew he was royalty, there was a chance he could negotiate. The way her eyes lit with greed as she examined his cock made him want to choke her.

"No ransom for you." She ignored the low laughter of the guard next to her.

Without thinking, Devnar took a step toward her and screamed in agony as her guard shot him with a pain amplifier. For an eternity, his world was filled with white-hot anguish as his nerves told his body he was burning alive. The distant screams of his men only added to his torment.

"Collar him," the woman said in a bored tone. "And the blond, and that one with the tattoo around his cock."

"What would you like us to do with the rest, Lady Grenba?"

Lady Grenba trailed past Devnar, and her skirts hissed along the floor as she inspected his four remaining men. Thank the Goddess the rest had managed to escape. "Kill them. Our agreement was only for the prince and to kill the rest, but I'm sure our friend won't mind if we keep these men as a bonus. After all, we sent them more than their fair share of women in our last shipment."

"No!" he screamed; then his lungs refused to work further as blinding pain sizzled through every nerve in his body. An eternity later, he twitched on the floor, his limbs still jerking with the aftershocks. Slowly his sight returned, and his raw throat convulsed as he tried to swallow.

A cool hand stroked his cheek. If he could have moved his body the slightest inch, he would have bitten those fingers off. "Did you feel the lust coming off of this one?" Lady Grenba's breath came out in a shudder. "With his royal blood, he will be the perfect gift to trap her. Exactly what she wants."

The greed in her words made him clench his teeth as rage fired through his muscles. "Fuck you," he managed to whisper as rough hands grabbed his body and jerked him upright.

Her hand was back again, tilting his chin upward. "Stupid man. Soon you'll be begging to please."

"Never." He would be damned if he'd let this bitch ride him. Goddess, he would give anything for the strength to reach out and snap her neck. Behind her, a guard dragged away the limp body of one of his men. A scorch mark on his temple confirmed his death, and Devnar was grateful it had been quick. He would mourn for them properly later; right now he had to take care of the living.

* * *

They clasped cold metal around his neck and wrists before he was thrown into a holding cell with his remaining men. The door sealed shut behind them, and he roared with fury. Naked and enraged, he found his men, Ikel and Bolin, watching him and tried to regain control of himself. Closing his eyes, he pulled himself up the wall as his limbs began to respond to the signals from his brain to move. He was their prince, and he was responsible for them. That thought pushed back the despair threatening to bury him.

Bolin slumped against the wall and clutched his head in his hands. "If the way that bitch looked at us is any indication, I think they plan to use us as studs. I'm not bonded. My soul isn't spoken for."

Panic tried to worm its way into Devnar's heart, and he turned Bolin's words over in his thoughts. To bond to a mate was a commitment that blended the souls of those two people together. They would be able to feel each other's emotions and sometimes thoughts. Their pleasure became your pleasure, their pain your pain. Once bonded, it was physically impossible to do anything that would hurt your bond mate. The thought of being forced to bond with someone he didn't love at once terrified and enraged him. His thoughts flashed to his sister and how she had been forced to bond with her rapists when she had been captured by the rebels but still managed to hold on to her sanity. He could only hope he had half her courage.

The sound of Ikel's knuckles cracking as he ground his fists together was loud in the little room. "If I have to service the same person over and over again, I won't be able to help bonding to them. I'll even want to do a blood exchange, beg them to be mine." Ikel looked up, and his voice cracked as he said, "With those hormones they're using, there's nothing that we can do to stop it. By the time a rescue comes, we won't want to leave."

The hopelessness of Ikel's words helped Devnar ground himself and turn his mind toward escape. "Do what you need to do to survive."

"What?" Ikel muttered a foul oath. "I'd rather cut my dick off than spend the rest of my life with a bitch like Lady Grenba."

"I'd sooner fuck a syphilitic warthog," Bolin added.

Grabbing Ikel's biceps in a punishing grip, Devnar said in a low voice, "You will do what you need to do to live. Fight them, make them pay for every time they use you, but do anything to survive." He released him and pressed their foreheads together, so close their breaths mingled. "And I promise you when we escape, we will kill any bitch—or bastard—that bonded you against your will."

Ikel shuddered and relaxed minutely, giving Devnar's shoulder a squeeze. "Volun will let everyone know of our capture. It will only be a matter of time before they send Lord Adsel to rescue us."

Giving him a bland look, Devnar gripped his collar and tugged until it gave him a small shock. "Who do you think betrayed us?"

Bolin stared at him and then slammed his fist into the wall. "That conniving, evil old bastard—"

"We don't know for sure." Ikel paced the confined space, each man trying to work off the arousal of the chemical scent and the battle lust that demanded a release.

"They were obviously waiting for us," Devnar snarled in frustration. "Someone tampered with our suits, and the Kyrimians knew exactly what mixture of hormones to use to immobilize us. Someone with access to our raiding vessel and knowledge of our route. Someone who pushed us into raiding today." The memory of Lord Adsel's snide remarks at court about not having the balls to provide his people with what they needed set his teeth on edge. When Volun showed up the next day saying he had received a tip about a Kyrimian ship loaded with zanthin, Devnar had leaped at the chance to prove Lord Adsel wrong and save his people.

"Do you think Volun betrayed us?"

Devnar rubbed his face. He wanted to believe his best friend had nothing to do with this, but right now anything was possible. "I-I don't think he did. But we can't rely on a rescue. We'll have to work on freeing ourselves."

"It shouldn't be too hard. Did you see those pretty-boy guards?" Ikel lifted his chin to an arrogant angle. "I've never heard of them engaging in open battle, always running back to the safety of their planet. They must not know how to fight."

"There's a good reason people don't want to fight them," Devnar added in a soft voice. "I've heard stories that they chemically neuter their captives. That they burn out the sex hormone receptors of their brains before using them as slaves on their moon trading posts."

"What?" Bolin pressed his legs together.

Ikel made a choking sound and cupped himself. "They won't do that to us, right? I mean, the way that bitch was looking at your cock, I thought she'd mount you right in the hallway."

"I knew I should have stayed home." Bolin slumped against the wall and slid down until he sat on the floor. "My mother wanted me to be a carpenter, but did I listen to her? Noooo, I had to go with the prince in search of women and glory."

"That's not going to happen to us." Devnar tried to put all his confidence as their commander and prince into his voice. "That bitch wants us intact for some reason. Use your heads, stay alive, and make them pay. I will get us out of this. On my honor as a prince of Jensia, I swear it."

His words visibly lifted his men's spirits, and he gave each a press on their shoulder before moving to the other side of the small room. Leaning back against the cold metal bench of the cell, Devnar prayed with all his might for his Goddess to give him the strength to get through this and seek his revenge.

Chapter Two

Melania Ophrim peered through the one-way glass and watched the man on the other side. His long, black hair hung thick and shining to the curve of his well-muscled shoulders. An elaborate tattoo covered the back of his right thigh and buttock. Scars traced over his body in no discernible pattern, and she wondered where he had been a worker.

The small viewing room had a few comfortable chairs pressed up against the far wall, but she chose to stand. Usually these rooms were used for training purposes, to watch a novice perform the skills they would need as a concubine without being intrusive. The one-way glass glowed with a running tally of statistics about the man standing on the other side, everything from his heart rate to the amount of pheromones he expelled with each breath.

"This is why you called me back from my vacation? He doesn't look like he needs my help." Her own reflection, dim and ghostly, superimposed over his. Long and straight, her light brown hair framed her heart-shaped face. The result of generations of careful breeding, she was beautiful enough to have been selected as a concubine and had the burning desires of that class.

Unfortunately the flaw of having one blue eye and one brown eye marked her as unfit to breed with royalty. That might have been overlooked due to the quality of her bloodline, but when her body attained womanhood, she had none of the lush curves or height that were considered the epitome of female perfection. Instead her breasts barely swelled at all, and her hips and bottom remained narrow and uncurved.

She was lucky to have not been sold at puberty to a whorehouse of the worker class. Instead her instinctual sensuality and iron self-control were used to help train those who had been given the great honor of being a concubine. That control now kept her pulse from racing at the disruption of her much needed downtime.

Unlike trainers, a breaker was forbidden orgasm with those they trained. Usually given novices who couldn't orgasm and enjoy themselves either because of abuse or shyness, a breaker needed all their compassion and skills focused solely on the novice. To seek their own orgasm would distract the breaker and turn the focus from the novice's pleasure to themselves.

Because of this, all her sexual frustration was bottled up until she spent weeks in a sexual frenzy with willing males trying to soothe the need for release. Not having an orgasm with her novices usually wasn't a problem. She specialized in helping novices and concubines who had been physically abused by careless Masters and Mistresses to heal enough to find pleasure in making love again. The man standing with his back to them had enough scars to have been abused, but their placement and shape didn't appear to be the result of torture.

More than that, the arrogant tilt of his shoulders and the way he carried himself spoke of great inner strength and confidence. There was none of the cringing, the effort to hide in the corner of the room that she associated with someone in need of her special skills. If anything, he radiated a dominance that brought an unwelcome flush of heat through her body. When she did have the luxury of indulging herself, she always chose males who were dominant and commanding. The giving up of control was as much of a rush for her as the actual sex.

Her gaze followed the curve of his waist, lingering on the heavy muscles of his thighs and the strength of his calves. Those muscles weren't shaped for beauty, but for physical labor. Was he one of the lucky workers who had won in the Arena and earned a chance to become a concubine?

Pimina moved next to her and crossed her arms in an uncharacteristic display of nerves. The head trainer of the Snowbound Pleasure House had been training concubines for over three hundred years. Melania examined her closely, noting the tightness of her still-full lips and the way she rubbed her fingertips against her elbows. They both wore the skintight black leather suits of trainers, but Pimina's had gold embellishments on the shoulders and Melania's had a hint of purple shimmer.

"You're my best breaker, and Lady Grenba requested you personally," Pimina said and glanced down at her. Small, even for a woman, Melania was used to people underestimating her because of her size and her ethereal looks. As a breaker, she counted on it.

Melania's lip curled in disgust at the mention of Lady Grenba's name. "I'm surprised the lady"—she spat the word out—"would want me anywhere near one of her novices again."

Not looking at her, Pimina needlessly flipped through various viewing screens, bringing up different angles and charts of the man in the room before her. "Yes, well, she seemed impressed that you were able to rehabilitate her last novice enough to be resold to another Mistress."

Hot and bitter, anger burned in Melania's gut as she remembered the months it had taken to rebuild the shattered man. With a sweet and submissive nature, he had suffered greatly at Lady Grenba's hands. A known sadist, she had hurt him and tortured him until he was almost catatonic. She and her trainer claimed they had no idea he wasn't a masochist and professed ignorance that he wasn't enjoying himself. Melania later learned the novice was kept constantly drugged so he was aroused, and gagged so he couldn't protest. She wanted to tell the regulators, but Pimina had warned her Lady Grenba would get a slap on the wrist while Melania would be signing her death warrant. Both she and the novice would be long dead before Lady Grenba came to any kind of trial.

Only the intervention of a kindhearted maid had alerted the trainers to his situation. He was given to Melania to heal, and Lady Grenba had escaped punishment by virtue of her royal blood. The maid had been punished for her intervention—nothing the regulators could have disciplined Lady Grenba for, instead, a horrible "accident" that left the maid maimed. She now worked for Melania after being removed from Lady Grenba's tender care.

"I spent months helping him to relearn the pleasure, the joy of service. Months holding him as he screamed and begged for death." She shuddered and took a deep breath. "Lady Grenba tried to have me sold to a whorehouse when I recommended to the regulators he not go back to her."

Silence settled over the room, and the air was thick with tension. Beyond the glass, the man turned to stare at them, and a slight smirk lifted his lips. Rough and masculine, his features held none of the carefully bred perfection of her people. It was almost shocking to see someone who wasn't faultless. Even at rest, his cock was long and thick enough to please any woman.

The edge of his firm upper lip lifted in a sneer filled with contempt. He said something in a dark and fluid language the computer had to translate for her to understand. *Conversion from Jensian to Kyrimian: I'll cut off your heads and shit down your throat.*

The offensive insult made her heart stutter in her chest as shock instantly slicked her body in stinging sweat. He switched to trader language and repeated the insult in words she could understand.

That wasn't any worker; in fact, he wasn't even of the same race. "Oh my Gods, he's an off-worlder. Pimina, we have to get him out of here! If the regulators find out—"

Pimina snapped, "Breaker, attend!"

The words of training sliced through her panic, and she sank to her knees with her palms turned up on her thighs. Legs pressed tightly together, she lifted her shoulders with a smooth indrawn breath and released a great deal of tension with her exhale. Hundreds of hours spent meditating in this pose did their job and helped her focus past her emotions.

"Better?" Pimina asked with a small smirk.

"Yes. Please forgive me for my unworthy display of panic."

Holding out her hand, Pimina helped Melania to her feet and said in a gentle tone, "Forgiven."

Melania leaned so close to the viewing screen, her breath fogged the glass. She stared at him in equal horror and fascination. "What is he doing here?"

"His name is Prince Devnar, and Lady Grenba captured him when he tried to raid her ship." Pimina waved her next question away. "That's not important. You are to train him and teach him the ways of the concubine."

"What? It is forbidden to train an off-worlder!" Most of the men and women who came through their pleasure house for training were willing volunteers, eager to earn the title of concubine and live the rest of their lives in comfort as beloved and treasured companions of their Master or Mistress.

A woman of her race was lucky to bear even one child in her lifetime. The royal houses married for power but chose their concubine for love. To sully the royal line with an off-worlder was treason, and the regulators would punish anyone who broke the law. Shaking her head, Melania backed away from the glass. "Pimina, we can be executed for smuggling him onto our world. Even if Lady Grenba brought him here." Her voice rose to a hysterical pitch. "This must be a trap; she must be trying to set us up. The regulators could be on their way here right now to—"

Pimina's long fingers tapped the viewing screen and called up his file. Melania gasped as the glittering crest of the empress shone before them, and Melania automatically dropped to her knees. Pimina's voice came out in a strained whisper. "His training is a royal decree."

Pimina opened his file on the viewing window, and Melania rose on shaky feet to read over the information. Everything in her own training told her instructing an off-worlder on how to be a concubine was wrong, blasphemy even. Regulations were very clear and strict on the sin of allowing any off-worlder onto Kyrimian soil.

The royal seal shimmered on the viewing glass, reminding her of the ancient videos of insects called fireflies that once inhabited their world before the Burning Times. Following the pattern of sparkles, she quickly came to a decision. If the empress had ordered it, she had less than no choice. Everyone knew even the regulators didn't dare go against the will of the empress, let alone a lowly breaker.

Pimina said in a dry voice, "His initial review has been a great disappointment. The only way we could get him to perform was to use heavy doses of an aphrodisiac, and even then he would refuse to orgasm."

Despite her fear and confusion, she couldn't help but be intrigued. "Any idea why?" The notion of fighting off an orgasm you were freely allowed and encouraged to have stunned her almost as much as seeing the empress's crest.

"No." Pimina's lips narrowed further, and Melania wondered if she had failed at getting the prince to perform. He was of no use as a concubine if he refused to serve with all the skill and finesse they would teach him. "His sexual profiles all came back strong, if not overly so. And look at his testosterone levels."

If she was reading his chart correctly, the lust he would give off would be amazing. Now she could see why the empress was willing to make an exception for him. Melania practically purred. Her race fed on the psychic energy given off by their partner during an orgasm. "Once properly trained..." Her breath came out in a shudder. "He'll be worth his weight in zanthin."

"Can you do it?" Pimina demanded and crossed her arms over her abundant chest. Taught to notice every nuance of a person's body language and appearance, Melania couldn't help but notice how Pimina's hands trembled. For some reason, that sign of nerves from the normally unflappable trainer bothered her more than anything else said here today.

She mustered her considerable inner strength and tried to reassure Pimina. "Of course."

The slight dropping of Pimina's shoulders sent a surge of pride through her at the trainer's trust in her abilities. Briefly closing her eyes, Melania focused herself on the off-worlder. If she was going to succeed, she had to start viewing him and treating him as any other reluctant novice.

Melania touched the window, flipping through the pages of his profile. He responded to females and males but performed unwillingly every time. Stubborn and arrogant, his temper had led to multiple punishments with the pain amplifier. He fought pleasure and did everything he could not to orgasm. No wonder his trainers had such a problem with him; they would have no idea how to handle someone who didn't want to learn a concubine's skills.

But breakers were trained to call forth passion from the shy or stubborn, and Melania was one of the best.

A thrill of desire moved through her as she watched him pace. She ruthlessly suppressed it. He was not meant for her, and she could not form an attachment to him. One of the reasons she made such a good breaker was because she was able to focus solely on the novice, not on her own needs and desires.

An elaborate tattoo sweeping over the broad muscles of his upper thigh caught her eye. What a magnificent challenge he would present. The chance to use her skills on a novice who might actually be used by the inner circle of the royal family made her mind race. Her shoulders fell, and she took a deep breath to try and center her thoughts. This wasn't about her needs; it was about his. She lived to serve.

"You have one month to break him." Pimina added this as if it was of no consequence.

"What?" Melania tore her eyes away from Devnar and stared at Pimina. "It takes months to do a proper breaking. I—"

"Don't tell me my craft!" Pimina clenched her hands into fists. "Lady Grenba plans on presenting him to the empress as a gift on her eighty-first birthday. The empress has been hinting she's looking for a new novice to replace her concubine who was assassinated. He won't be the only one presented to her, you can be sure of that."

Melania rubbed her mouth with the back of her hand. "So the empress is finally ready to break her mourning. Can we be sure he will be well received?"

"Lady Grenba wouldn't risk the insult of giving her an unwanted gift. Or waste such a valuable novice." Pimina smoothed back a stray curl from Melania's face. "He is a unique present the lady went to great trouble to secure on the empress's behalf. There have been rumors the empress wants to open Kyrimia to off-worlders."

Melania carefully sat in one of the comfortable cream chairs. If Pimina kept throwing shocks at her like this, she might as well sit down before she fell down. "The regulators will never allow that." Looking at the man pacing on the other side of the glass, she repeated the first rule of regulation. "Off-worlders are treacherous monsters that want to rape what is left of our mother planet. They are forbidden."

Pimina's lips twitched with unsaid words before she blew out a breath. "Well, physically he doesn't appear monstrous. Besides, those decisions are the realm of royal politics and out of our hands. The best we can do is deal with the problem or opportunity given to us." She handed Melania the control bracelet keyed to the prince's collar and cuffs. "Lady Grenba mentioned the empress is very much looking forward to meeting him and will be very disappointed if we don't succeed in making him into a presentable concubine."

"So you're saying if we don't train him and word reaches the empress of our failure, we should sell all of our possessions and start running." Melania ran her suddenly slick hands down the liquid black fabric of her breakers suit. No one denied the empress her desires and lived.

Pimina gave a rough laugh that held a ragged edge of fear. "If we fail, we won't have to worry about the empress. Lady Grenba has promised she'll personally eliminate our entire bloodline."

Though she never knew her parents—they had abandoned her as soon as the flaw of her different colored eyes became apparent—she still winced. "Anything else I need to know?" She almost managed to keep the tremor out of her voice.

Devnar turned his back to them, the angle and posture of his shoulders clearly displaying his contempt. If she didn't know better, she would think he could see and hear them.

"Be wary of him. Restrain him at all times. He snapped one of the trainer's arms after she tried to mount him." Melania gaped at her, and Pimina quickly continued. "He was highly drugged and unaware of what he did, but he didn't regret it once he sobered up. So no drugs and always restrain him."

Melania stood and walked back over to the window, her gaze switching between the man behind the glass and information on the screen. She tapped the open file on the window with a long, purple-tinted nail and read the report about the assault. She hated to use restraints and force, but the thought of broken bones didn't appeal to her either. "Anything else I need to know?" she said in a dry voice.

Pimina hesitated and evaluated Melania with all her attention. "If you succeed, and he is chosen by the empress, you will be allowed to have your own concubine."

The world flashed white before her eyes, and her heart gave a painful pound in her chest. Next to her, Pimina muttered an oath and held her as she sagged. "My own?"

Pimina released her, then stepped back. Instead of meeting Melania's look, Pimina kept her gaze on the man on the other side of the viewing glass. "It has been decreed that whatever trainer or breaker provides the empress with her next concubine will be allowed to have a concubine of their own."

With her palms against the glass, Melania stared at the man who was the key to all her oldest dreams. A concubine of her own to love and cherish, someone to come home to, someone to fill the cold void in her heart that yearned for a mate to call her own.

"Pay attention, Breaker." Melania tried not to squirm underneath that hard gaze, but it quickly brought her back to the time when she was trained by Pimina. "His people might attempt a rescue since he is a prince. I doubt they would make it onto our planet, but you never know. Make sure your stables are well guarded, and don't lose your focus. If he escapes, Lady Grenba will destroy you. Even I will not be able to save your life." Her voice grew soft, and she gave Melania a brief hug. "You'll never have a chance like this again."

"As if spending the next five hundred years in a pain amplifier wasn't enough motivation." Melania laughed and rubbed her hands together briskly to work away the residue of fear. His race was a complete mystery to her, and she didn't know how heightened his senses were. A thrill washed through her as she realized she would be the first breaker to ever work with his people. "When should I begin?"

"Now." Pimina cupped her cheek and gave her a rare smile. "You have always been my best breaker, Melania. I know your family curses those eyes that kept you out of service, but I do not doubt for a minute you would have made a wonderful concubine."

Melania blushed at the compliment. "Thank you."

A ghost of apprehension swam through Pimina's stern gaze. "Do not fail me."

"I won't." She lifted her chin and strode toward the door leading to the room that held Devnar. She prayed she would find the strength to break him and save herself.

Chapter Three

The metal of the collar around Devnar's neck vibrated a warning when his impatient strides took him too close to the window overlooking the garden. He ground his teeth and backed away from the murky patch of late-afternoon sunlight and turned his anger on the viewing window. On the other side of the glass, he knew those bitches were watching him.

Baring his teeth in what could never be mistaken for a smile, he resumed his pacing. At least a week had passed since his capture. Every day was worse than the one before. The constant sexual assault on his senses was taking its toll, and he didn't know how much longer he could last.

He selected a piece of fruit from a silver bowl and took a viscous bite, wishing it was the throat of his last trainer. That stupid bitch had learned the hard way not to push him too far. He felt a brief pang of remorse at having hurt her, but it was quickly buried beneath his well-cultivated rage. As long as he was angry, he could distance himself from bonding.

The fresh burst of sweet juice cleared his palette, and he found himself eating down to the core out of habit. The decadence and luxury of this place further grated on his nerves. Everything was about indulgence and pleasure here, and he fought from being seduced by it.

He tossed the remains of the core on the floor in a useless act of defiance and wished they would hurry and do whatever they'd brought him here for. Bathed and oiled, he was told he was going to meet his breaker, whatever the hell that was. The word itself was intimidating, but he wasn't going to let them scare him. Last time he had refused to perform, his captors had threatened to send him to a breaker, and he had laughed in their faces. Their shock had added to his enjoyment, and he'd told them all the foul things he planned on doing to this "breaker" before they gagged him and sent him back to his cell.

The only joy he got out of his day was watching those bitches and bastards gnash their teeth in frustration as his body denied their orders. Oh, they could make him fuck using the aphrodisiac, but they couldn't force him to come. It was steadily getting harder to resist. All that sexual frustration was going to have to be released, either in passion or violence, like the explosion of rage that had led to him hurting that trainer.

If only he could figure out what they wanted with him, aside from his cock. There had to be some reason he was here besides being used as a stud. From what he had seen, there was no lack of willing novices and concubines with perfect features and bodies eager to serve.

The door next to the viewing glass slid open, and he unconsciously assumed a fighting stance. The breath left his lungs in a soft hiss at the sight of his new breaker. She was stunning. Well, they were all stunning, but something about her called to him, and he hated her on sight for making him feel this way.

Tiny and perfectly formed, her shiny nutmeg brown hair fell bone straight to the slightly rounded curve of her bottom. Small breasts pressed against the black leather of her uniform, and he noted an unfamiliar purple sheen to all that darkness. Following the line of her body, he was captured by her gaze. One of her eyes was the clear blue of the summer sky on his planet, while the other was as brown as dark chocolate.

Curiosity, fear, and heat flickered across her face, and he was glad to note that she was easy to read. They stared at each other. Her expression settled on determination. The small lines around her mouth deepened as she firmed her full lips and tightened her jaw.

Trying to get as much information on her as he could, he took in a deep breath of her scent. Healthy female with a slight edge of fear. His protective instincts roared to life and demanded he defend her from whatever made her afraid. Too bad it was probably him. He cursed his biology's blind desire to find the perfect mate and conjured images of battle to turn his mind from sex.

"Hello, Novice." Her voice was deep and husky instead of the high pitch he expected from such a small and delicate woman. Rather than acknowledge her, he selected some grapes from the bowl and began to eat them. Her unusual eyes followed the movements of his mouth, and he spit a seed at her feet.

The faintest quirk of her firm pink lips showed her amusement at his insult. With a bored look, she pointed to her feet. "Attend."

Yawning, he wandered over to the window again and steeled his body against the warning buzz of the collar. Before he made it three steps, pain shot through him and brought him to his knees. With a groan, he strained to lift his head as her small feet moved across the carpet and stopped in front of him.

"I don't know what your past trainers let you get away with, but you will obey me." She tipped his chin with the toe of her boot, and he glared up at her. No emotion on her face, but the spice of her musk flavored the air. "Do you understand?"

Knowing he was being foolish but unable to stop himself, he jerked his head away and snarled at her. Her perfectly arched eyebrows rose in surprise before she purposefully let her finger hover over the control bracelet. His anger gave him the strength to curve his hands into fists like he was going to attack her. The only warning he had was the flash of regret on her face before another searing bolt of agony had him flat on his back at her feet.

As he panted, he struggled to hide his smile. She didn't like inflicting pain and would hesitate before punishing him. In the future, he could use that against her to help him escape.

"Devnar." He at once hated and loved the way his name sounded in her husky voice. "My name is Melania, and I am your breaker."

Not wanting to spend the rest of the day writhing on the floor, he propped himself to his knees and glared. "That's *Prince* Devnar, you bitch." Her soft chuckle raised the hair on his arms. "What the hell is a breaker?"

Using the toe of her boot again, she pressed it on the back of his head and forced his face to the ground. Anger surged through him, and he fought against the urge to flip her on her back and force her to acknowledge him as the dominant. As long as he wore the slave collar, he had no choice.

"I am going to break you of your useless and stupid pride keeping you from fulfilling your potential as a concubine." Her tone made it obvious she actually thought she was doing him a favor.

The pressure of her foot lifted from his head, and her delicate hand stroked back his hair from his cheek. He fought the arousal her touch brought him and gritted his teeth. Her hand in his hair tightened; then she quickly released him and stepped back. Even with his head pressed to the carpet, he could smell the surge in her desire.

He turned his head and watched the shine of her boots as she strode over to the mirror wall. She tapped on the glass twice before saying, "Have him washed and brought to my stables."

In a show of defiance, he pushed himself from the floor and stood despite the lack of strength in his legs. His muscles shivered, but he refused to stay on the floor any longer. Amusement was evident in the slight curve of her full lips as she examined him. "Also I want his nipples pierced."

"What?" he barked out and fisted his hands together.

"Your nipples." She moved to stand in front of him and ran her delicate fingers down his chest. "You have lovely nipples, and I want them pierced." Watching him carefully, she ran her fingertips over each nub, and they hardened beneath her touch. He squeezed his eyes shut and tried to think of something other than the sensation of her working him with gentle pulls. Being so aroused by his enemy humiliated him, yet he couldn't pull away from her touch.

"Look at how hard they get," she whispered against his chest. "How they respond to my touch." The musky scent of her lust assaulted his instincts, and blood rushed to his cock in a hard throb. He forced his eyes open and glared at her. She could make his body respond, but she couldn't make him enjoy it.

"They get hard when I take a shit too. Don't flatter yourself."

Now she did smile and gave his sensitized nipples a hard yank. "Does your cock get hard when you defecate? Will we have to experiment with someone sucking you while you empty your bowels?"

His jaw dropped, and she turned her head slightly at the *hiss* of the door opening. She released his body and stepped back with an appreciative murmur as she unabashedly stared at his erection. His self-disgust grew as his cock throbbed and grew harder beneath her gaze. Too bad his prick didn't care about his mental distress; it wanted to bury itself in that breaker's hot cunt.

Two servants appeared in the doorway and waited with impassive faces. He ignored them as much as they ignored him while they escorted him out of the room. Even if he managed to overpower them, his collar crippled his body with agony as soon as he reached a door or window he wasn't authorized to use. He'd made that painful discovery the first day he'd landed on this polluted rock.

After passing through a series of archways and rooms, a final door opened, and he was quickly hustled into a waiting transporter. Even the threat of his collar couldn't stop him from planting his feet and attempting to get a look at something other than walls. He turned his face to the sky and tried to catch a glimpse of blue. All that met his gaze were the dirty, gray-green clouds that seemed to constantly shroud the sun.

A daily bath in artificial sunlight kept him healthy, but he missed the scent of growing things and the warmth of true light. His people spent most of their time outdoors among the giant trees and vast inland lakes of his world. To be kept in a small room day after day had come closer to breaking him than any other mental tricks his captors had tried.

A snarl escaped his lips as they shoved him into the small pod, but the door closed before he could do anything more. The walls went opaque, and he lurched as the transporter began to move. The padded seat cradled his body as he closed his eyes and tried to keep the image of long, brown hair and pink lips out of his mind.

* * *

Later that evening, Devnar hung suspended against a wall in the vast dining room of Melania's estate, watching her eat dinner. The metal cuffs around his wrist were held against the wall by powerful magnets, spreading his arms at his sides but not high enough to impede his circulation. A man who had identified himself as Devnar's groom had washed every inch of him until he had been cleaned in places even his most ardent lover hadn't explored. The groom had added ankle cuffs as well when Devnar called one of the maids every foul thing he could think of after she had pinched his ass.

His nipples still throbbed from where they had been pierced, but the cellular reconstruction cream was doing its job and healing him rapidly. The gold rings glinted in the subdued lighting. As a maid walked past him, her full skirt brushed his legs and he snarled at her. To his disgust, she didn't even flinch or disturb the bottle of wine she carried to the table.

Soft music played in the background, and a jungle of plants lined the walls. The tall trees reaching toward the dark skylights made his heart ache for his home. He attempted to shift into a more comfortable position in his shackles and resumed his glaring at Melania.

A gold mesh loincloth covered his groin, but it left little to the imagination. His hair was now back in a tight braid that hung over his shoulder, and his skin had been oiled until it gleamed. Even his body hair had been waxed and groomed until he barely recognized himself.

Raising the last bite of her dinner to her mouth, Melania sighed and patted her lips with her cloth napkin. Despite himself, he was fascinated by her.

Every move she made was with a grace and control that turned a simple meal into an erotic dance.

Though she hadn't acknowledged him once, he still felt she was putting on a show for his benefit. Too bad it was a wasted effort. Yeah, the pressure in his balls wasn't from watching those pink lips wrap around the fork and suck the food off. Not at all.

"Tell me about your home world, Prince." Her mouth parted as she raised an etched wineglass to her lips, and he had a sudden mental image of those pink lips parting to take his cock down her slender throat. She regarded him over the rim with open curiosity as he tried to banish that thought from his mind.

Unsure of her motivation, he lifted his lip in a silent snarl. "It's better than this piss hole you call a planet. Why you waste your time guarding this polluted hunk of rock is beyond me. Who would want to invade a world where you have to live beneath domes to survive?"

Gently placing the wineglass back on the table, she toyed with the stem, and her eyebrows drew together. He was amazed at how easy she was to read. She didn't try to hide any of her emotions from him…or she was a far better liar than he thought.

"How do your people live?"

"Why do you care? I'm a prisoner to fuck and punish."

She crossed her slender legs and leaned back into the chair. Her foot tapped an irritated dance in the air, though her voice was still calm. "I've never met an off-worlder before." She hesitated, and the tempo of her foot picked up. "My education did not include lessons about other worlds."

With a snort, he jerked at his bonds. "Why would they bother to educate a whore?"

Oh, that made her mad.

Her full, pink lips grew narrow, and her foot stopped, the tip pointing at the ceiling. "Obviously you know no more about my culture than I do about yours. I am a breaker, a trainer of concubines."

She went silent again and stroked her fingertips over her lips. His gaze followed the progress of her finger, and he wished it was the head of his cock pressing against that soft flesh. What would it be like to have her mouth wrapped around him? Would she swallow his seed, or would she want it to cover her face?

He startled as she rose from her chair, jerked out of his daydreams by the liquid flash of her leather beneath the subdued lighting. He bit his tongue and willed his body not to respond to her. She was the enemy, a bitch like the rest. The soft roll of her hips as she strode across the pale wood floor toward him set his teeth on edge.

"You are my novice, and you should be thankful for the chance to ever serve a royal house."

"I am a prince. I am no one's whore." He raised his chin and stared down his nose at her as she slowly walked past the edge of the table, trailing her fingers down the polished wood.

"No, you're a lucky fool." Her scent saturated the air as she gave him a look of disapproval that, strangely, hurt his feelings. He must be losing his mind. Only a crazy man would give a shit about what his beautiful, soft, and delicious adversary thought about him. "By all rights you should be spending your days in the zanthin mines with the rest of the thieves and murderers."

"I'm not a murderer." He ignored her snort. "The only men I've ever killed were on the field of battle in honorable combat." Why was he trying to defend himself to this slut? Why should he care what she thought of him? The fact that she was the first person to treat him with any hint of kindness since his capture didn't mean she wasn't here for the purpose of making him a compliant slave.

As he grappled with his confused feelings, she leaned close enough for her breath to warm his chest. So tiny he could crush her with one hand. The mental fantasy of hurting her didn't bring him any of the pleasure it used to when he'd dreamed of torturing his other trainers. His lust refused to be turned to battle rage and deepened as her heat moved over his exposed skin like the sunlight he craved.

"Your people like to fight?" The sensation of her breath caressing his skin made the hair on his arms stand on end.

"No one likes war. We fight to protect our people, to keep our territory and women out of the hands of the southern rebels." He tried to shift away from her fingertips as they traced the ridges of his abdominal muscles. Little sparks of pleasure followed her touch, and his cock twitched with interest.

"Then our people have something in common." She pressed the soft pads of her fingers into the hard curve of his hip bone.

"What are you talking about? We're nothing like you." His heartbeat sped as she toyed with the top edge of his loincloth.

"Really? Aren't you like those rebels you protect your home against? Didn't you raid what you hoped was an innocent vessel in order to pillage it?"

Her words struck him, and he snapped, "That's not the same at all. We raid to survive. Look at you; look at this place." He gestured to the room with his shackled hand. "I bet you've never gone hungry, never known what it's like to wonder where your next meal is coming from. You've probably never even seen a starving child, let alone had to hold one while they died in your arms." His breath came out in harsh pants, and he fought to control himself. He had no need to justify himself to this bitch. Why the hell did he care if she thought he was scum? As soon as he could, he was going to get out of here and kill anyone who tried to stop him, even her.

Ignorant of his internal struggle, she placed her hand gently over his heart. "And you have?" Instead of anger, her voice held a pity that scraped against his nerves. "I'm so sorry you had to go through that. It must haunt you." The memory of the massive droughts that had led to the hungry years poked at the ache in his heart. He fought against the soothing effect of her husky voice as the perfume of her arousal filled his nose. "Whether you believe it or not, Prince, it is hard for me to watch you or anyone else suffer. I will do everything in my power to make this as easy and pleasurable for you as I can. I promise."

The muscle in his jaw twitched as he clenched his teeth and stared over her head at the wall. A cascade of water fell in undulating sheets of color from somewhere in the ceiling, illuminated from below by shifting lights. Green shimmers blended to violet as she stood before him, her breath tickling his chest. Slowly the regrets of the past faded until he was once again focused entirely on her.

Soft and warm, her hand cupped his cheek and stroked his skin. Feminine, fragile, compassionate, she brought all his protective instincts to the surface, and he tried to fight his primal nature. Though he'd never experienced it himself, the signs of his body reacting to a potential mate scared him. Even now he responded to her nearness with an eager rush of lust that tightened his balls.

"My servants told me you were a good boy about your piercings." She ignored his swearing, and he could smell a faint hint of her musk. So she wasn't as unaware of him as she pretended. The thought pleased him, and he cursed his own stupidity. She held him captive and kept him from his people. The fact that her hot little cunt got wet for him shouldn't stroke his ego; it should disgust him. And he certainly shouldn't be fantasizing about how her pussy would taste on his tongue. "For that you get a reward."

"I want nothing from you," he said in a low growl and jerked at his bonds.

She pulled out a small vial attached to a silver chain from beneath her leather uniform. As she held his gaze, she pulled out the stopper and the scent of a female in heat reached him.

"Slut," he snarled out. Goddess, how he hated that they used that scent to make him perform. The delicious scent should be coming from a real woman, not some lab. He was glad she didn't know her own natural scent affected him as strongly as the synthetic.

She capped the vial without using it and let it lay against the small swell of her breasts. Her lips pursed as she studied his expression, and he tried not to squirm. For Goddess sake, he could snap her in half. There was no reason he should feel intimidated by her gaze.

"If you can perform without the stimulant, I won't use it. The choice is yours."

Blinking at her, he tried to process her words. This was the first time anyone had offered him a choice, and he didn't know how to react. His body certainly wanted the woman on her knees before him. He had become accustomed to the constant efforts to arouse him, and as a result, his body was producing more sexual hormones than ever. It was a natural response to feeding the constant sensual hunger of a breeding female.

Without another word, she ripped off the golden cloth covering his groin. Her strange bicolored gaze never left his, and he tried to keep from looking away. Her pupils dilated, and her lips softened a fraction. Blood rushed to her cheeks and gave them a soft pink tint.

The aroma of her excitement reached his nose, and he stifled a groan. Already his body surged at her unique smell, and that meant trouble. He closed his eyes and tried to sever the connection she had with him. It didn't help. Now he could smell her even more, and his body throbbed with the need to ease her desire.

He could almost feel her small hands playing with his nipples. That last thought brought his eyes open with a flash, and he found his imagination hadn't lied to him. Her fingers were gently pulling at the golden rings as she watched him.

"Get your hands off of me," he said in low growl.

"No." She tugged harder, and her nostrils flared.

He jerked against his bonds, a useless fight in every way. With the pad of her fingertips, she slowly traced each nipple, gently moving the hoop through his skin. Each touch was measured and controlled, skilled in a way that left him breathless.

"You are mine to play with," she whispered against his chest, her lips trailing over his skin. "I will give you pleasure like you never imagined. All I ask in return is your complete obedience. Let yourself go; let me make the decisions. The only thing I want you to do is feel."

He clenched his hands into fists and gave her a glare that had reduced grown men to tears. Instead of being scared, she licked her lower lip in a gesture that left it soft and wet. Just like he imagined her pussy was, trapped beneath her leathers.

He turned his head to the side; he refused to give her the satisfaction of watching what her touch did to him. It felt damned good. He never would have anticipated those small hunks of metal in his nipples could bring him so much pleasure. "I belong to no one."

The soft breath of her laughter moved to the sensitive skin on the side of his ribs. "You're mine until I say otherwise." She punctuated her words with a sharp tug on his nipple.

"Bitch," he whispered. Her leather-clad hips brushed his erection, and he shook with the need to press into her.

"I can taste your desire," she said in her husky voice. "It's like candy on my tongue."

Her mouth latched on to his nipple, playing with the ring and breaking his self-control. Even as he thrust against her, he cursed himself for his weakness. The tip of her clever tongue soothed his aching flesh, and he strained against his bonds.

She pulled back, and he instantly missed her lips on him. "Look at me."

Spice and musk radiated from her now. She was so ready for him. He bet the crotch of her leather suit was soaked with her juices. It really irritated him that on the outside, she could appear so calm and poised. Deliberately he turned his head away from her and stared at the floral arrangement at the other side of the room.

Laughter greeted his defiance and angered him further. With a husky purr, she closed her hand around his cock and gave it a hard squeeze. "Look at me."

He somehow managed to keep his head turned even as his erection thrust into her palm. Soft as silk, her skin brought all the nerves in his prick to life. Slowly she stroked him in silence until his sac drew tight and his body slammed into her small fist.

Goddess, he wanted to bend her over and fuck her in the worst way.

Her hand moved away, leaving him straining against the air as his cock ached for release.

"Look at me."

The deep throb in his balls tormented him almost as much as her scent. "No."

"Devnar," she murmured and pressed her body fully against his. "I'm not doing this to torment you. I'm doing this to free you of yourself."

"You're doing this because it excites you," he spat out and turned to look at her as she jumped back from him. "You said you can taste my desire? Well, I can smell your hot cunt from across the room."

She gaped at him, a faint blush staining her pale cheeks. It was the first real expression he had ever seen from her.

"That's right. I can smell how much you want me." He rolled his hips, and her gaze darted to his cock before flashing back up to his face.

"I must have spilled some of the aphrodisiac." She squared her shoulders and tried to regain her footing. Satisfaction quirked his lips into a smile as she attempted to lie to herself. The other trainers hadn't hidden their arousal from him, but then again, they hadn't been breakers. He had no idea why the thought of being aroused by him embarrassed her, but he would try to exploit what he perceived to be a weakness. She certainly hadn't been self-conscious when she'd suckled his nipples and made his prick want to explode.

"I'm looking at you," he taunted. "Why don't you come over here and finish what you started." Her nostrils flared, and he laughed. "Imagine how good I would taste if you could actually make me come."

This broke her indecision, and she grabbed his aching cock hard in her fist. "You will come when I say you will."

Not responding to her threat, he rocked his erection in and out of her fist. This was going so wrong so fast, but he was helpless to stop. She remained frozen before him, watching his cock shuttle through her slender fingers, unable to fully grip his girth. So beautiful. He wanted to bury his hands in that amazing long hair and come all over her face.

She took a deep breath and loosened her grip so only the barest friction was there. He growled deep in his throat and ordered, "Finish me."

"Beg for it," she replied and held his gaze.

"Fuck you," he said and then groaned as her touch turned featherlight. He followed her hand as she removed it from his aching cock and slowly licked her palm. The shocking pink of her tongue had him sucking in his breath. When her slick palm stroked him, he threw his head back and tried to pull the magnets holding his wrists out of the wall. Faster now, she played with his prick with a deft touch that left him panting and sweating. Even the pleasure slaves they had used on him hadn't known how to work his body like this little female did.

She'd bring him to the edge, then pull back and leave him one good jerk away from coming. His balls really did ache now, and he wanted nothing more than to empty himself all over her. To mark her with his scent and make her his. That thought should have alarmed him, but he was past caring. All his attention focused on the female and what she was doing to his body.

"Suck me, and I'll beg." There, it wasn't quite begging. In fact he was making her do something. Yeah, right.

Her breath came out in a soft rush. "Beg me."

He couldn't give in, he couldn't let her—those thoughts shattered as her other incredibly soft hand stroked his sac. "Please."

"Not good enough."

Gritting his teeth, he shook a drop of sweat out of his eye. His whole body gleamed with a mixture of sweat and oil as his cock throbbed in pain. "Please, Melania. Please make me come. Let me empty myself down that pretty throat."

She sagged against him and slid down his body, her small and firm leather-clad breasts brushing over his cock. Only the thought of her mouth wrapped around him kept him from coming right then and there. "Touch yourself," he panted as her breath stirred the hair at the base of his cock.

"It is forbidden," she murmured one second before engulfing his length in the tight heat of her mouth.

All rational thoughts left his mind as he cried out. So fucking good. Her velvet-soft tongue lapped at him as she sucked him with a skill that made him writhe in his bindings. He wanted to make it last, wanted to draw this extreme pleasure out.

Her hands dug into his ass and pulled him closer. Dimly he noted they shook, but even that thought fled as she groaned around his length. Her small but surprisingly strong hands held him still, and she slowly worked him deeper into her mouth until she had to open her throat for him.

That did it. The sensation of the muscles of her throat fluttering around the tip of his cock and her hands holding him still drove him over the edge. He threw his head back and felt his orgasm boil from his balls and flow out in hard spurts.

She swallowed each jet of cum, drinking him down with a greed that bordered on violence. At last she released him with a long suck that had him bucking against her. Unable to fully support his weight, he sagged in his shackles and watched her as she remained on her knees, panting and shivering with soft groans. Why she didn't give herself the orgasm she so obviously needed was beyond him.

"Bitch," he said in a pleasure-slurred voice. "You enjoyed eating my cum, didn't you?"

She stood on unsteady feet and avoided his gaze. Her voice was rough with desire, and the waves of need coming off her sent a rush of blood to his cock. "Someone will be back to unchain you and feed you. I want you well rested for tomorrow."

The way she shifted her stance, keeping her legs tightly pressed together, confirmed his suspicion. She wanted him badly, but for some reason couldn't have him. Maybe the breakers were forbidden from having their release with him. If that was true, he could use that to torment her until she made a mistake.

Chapter Four

The dim, early-morning sun burned off the last of the artificial dew from the soft green grass of Melania's private garden. High, dark stone walls decorated with flowering vines enclosed the garden, while a clear dome above kept it secure. A synthetic breeze blew through the manicured trees and stirred the loose strands of hair against her cheek. Normally she delighted in coaxing a shy pleasure slave into a screaming orgasm in the broad daylight of her gardens. Now she hesitated and steeled herself for the mental battle ahead.

Each flower and plant was carefully pruned and bred for perfection, making the contrast of Devnar's scarred body suspended between two smooth magnetic stone pillars all the more startling. She knew he was aware of her presence. His big shoulders tensed as she approached, and the hem of her black leather gown dragged across the grass with a hiss.

She closed her eyes and fought for self-control. She had to break him, had to make him into a concubine fit for an empress. Becoming addicted to his orgasm was not an option. He had filled her dreams, tormenting her body until she woke burning on the edge of release a dozen times. Beyond that, he intrigued her. A good breaker knew the mind and soul of their novice, but his life and personality were a mystery to her. Truth be told, she was afraid to know anything more about him. Afraid she would become further ensnared by her growing obsession.

He was the key to having a concubine. She kept repeating that mantra, picturing a dark-haired man who looked disturbingly like Devnar waiting in bed for her. With her resolve strengthened, she hurried toward him before she even made the conscious decision to move.

"Good morning, pet." She ran her hand over his lower back, admiring the play in his muscles as he struggled not to flinch. The sun brought out the tattoo across his thigh that dipped over the curved muscle of his butt. She longed to run her tongue over each intricate swirl.

"Bitch."

With a soft laugh, she continued to touch him as she ducked beneath his spread arms and around to his front. Heat rushed through her blood and tightened her core as she noted he was already fully erect. Instead of looking at her, he kept his eyes focused on the fountain behind her.

"What do these markings mean?" She traced the tips of her nails over his muscled flank, following the sweep of the tattoo as it wrapped around his thigh.

He pressed his lips together in a firm line that would have looked petulant if his face wasn't so rugged. As it was, it looked like he had eaten a lemon.

She bit her lower lip to suppress a giggle and gently toyed with his nipple ring. His erection bobbed with each tug of the ring, and she had to resist the urge to sink to her knees and take its delicious length in her mouth. "If you tell me, I won't have your cock pierced without your permission."

He coughed and stared at her while the pulse in the side of his neck throbbed. "It's the mark of my royal heritage. The circles show who my ancestors were, and the curves represent my accomplishments on the battlefield."

A warrior, of course. The warriors of her world came only from the working class. She never had any interaction with them other than the occasional merchant. The classes were forbidden from mingling, and the regulators enforced the rule with no mercy.

He watched her trace a curving pattern on his thigh and said in a low voice, "The swirls are the mark of favor from my Goddess."

Another small piece to his personality fell into place. She stroked the twisting whirls of black and white with a gentle touch. His muscles jumped beneath her hand like a skittish animal. What would it be like to know where you came from? To be able to name your family and share in their love?

"Now get your peasant hands off of me. If we were on my planet, I would kill you for touching me."

The bitterness in his voice jerked her back to the present. Deliberately, she rested her palm above the jutting length of his erection. The hard muscles of his lower abdomen tightened, and she stroked the ridges. He refused to meet her look and stared at the fountain again. For all his protests, his body wanted to serve.

Wanted her.

After a lifetime of being considered ugly, she thrilled at the knowledge that he found her attractive...desirable. The way he looked at her, even when he was angry, made her heart beat faster.

Irritated at the possessive turn of her thoughts, her words held more anger than she'd intended. "I don't know what kind of primitive rutting your people do on your planet, but today I'm going to teach you how to pleasure a woman."

Now he met her look, and he wasn't happy. So much fire in that gaze, so much strength bound for her pleasure. She gave herself a mental shake and tried to distance her mind from her body's desires. She was a breaker; it was not her place to find pleasure in this. She lived to serve and for the pleasures of others. Her only hope of ever having a mate and family of her own rested in making this male fit for the empress.

She had no other choice.

Repeating this mantra, she attempted to focus on his body with an objective eye. Despite his anger, he was still so hard the veins of his cock stood out in sharp relief. That was good, but if he displayed this temper to the empress, she would have him killed. The thought stung her heart more than it should, and she moved so the shiny black leather of her dress brushed his legs.

"Don't touch me," he growled, and her body shivered in response.

"Pet, I can do anything I want. You are mine." She emphasized her words by stroking the line of his jaw and over to his lips. A little scar marred the full lower one, and she mused that it would have to be removed before he was presented to the empress. Too bad, because that small flaw accented the curve of his mouth.

Distracted by her admiration, she didn't notice his jaw tensing until it was too late and he had her finger trapped between his teeth. Her breath caught in her throat as he bit down, and she cursed herself for letting her mind wander. Every moment of her life would be unending pain if she failed at her task. With a slow, gentle movement of her hand, she stroked against his chest. She could use the sting of the shock collar, but that wouldn't teach him anything. He needed to respond to her, to bend to her will and want to please.

"Very nice," she purred and pressed herself closer. The pressure of his bite increased, and she relaxed into it. Pain could be pleasure, and if she was reading him right, he wouldn't go any further than this. The more she showed she enjoyed it, the more confused and uncertain he became.

The hesitant tip of his tongue flicked over her trapped finger, and heat raced through the nerves of her body to her clit. She had spent half the night masturbating to the memory of his body, and it hadn't been enough. She stood on her tiptoes and wiggled her hips so the slit in the front of her skirt parted; then the head of his cock touched the curls of her pussy. Desire surged through her, and she wanted with all her heart to wrap her legs around his waist and ride his magnificent erection.

With a grunt, he let go of her finger and shuddered in his bonds. "Get away from me."

"No." She traced her lips over his jaw. A faint hint of stubble rasped along her mouth. The tip of his cock pressed into the curve of her hip as he thrust forward. Fire, she was playing with fire.

She licked the seam of his lips, then sighed. He tasted wonderful, masculine and rich with passion. The chemical rush of his desire made her lean into his mouth, eager to tease more of a delicious reaction from him. All her nerves blazed to life, and her skin became extra sensitive.

"I don't want you," he whispered against her lips. The motion of his words turned into a kiss, each sound slow and thick with need. "Stop."

So tempting. She wanted to lose herself in his mouth. Her delicate arms wrapped around his neck, and she pulled back with a sigh. "Why do you fight it? I can feel your desire, your need wrapping like an iron fist around your cock."

"I don't want you," he repeated and tried to pull his hips away. Shame, desire, and anger battled in his gaze before he looked over her head and back to the fountain.

Lifting the edges of her skirts, she fastened them back behind her so her body was framed by the black leather. The top still hid her breasts, but the breeze cooled the moisture coating her inner thighs. His nostrils twitched, and his big hands fisted above the shiny silver metal of his cuffs.

She was glad they were alone. Evidence of her desire would have been enough to have him reassigned to a different breaker and her sold to a worker class brothel where anyone could buy her body. Her own need was a distraction she couldn't afford. She must be solely focused on him instead of giving in to her own fierce cravings. The thought of her failure should have filled her with shame; instead she felt an unfamiliar sensation of defiance. Heady and frightening, it sped her pulse. The mixture of her body's response to her desire and the almost drugging effect of his need made her reckless.

As she struggled to regain the upper hand, she strolled over to the fountain and sat on the edge. His gaze followed her, and she parted her legs, displaying herself to him. The tip of his tongue licked his lips as he tried to look away while she traced one finger down the seam of soft skin where her inner thigh met her pussy. Her mind clamored at her to stop before it was too late, but her body urged her onward. Just this little bit of relief. It wasn't like she was actually going to be coming with him.

She tried to convince herself she was only doing this to arouse him as she cupped her mound and arched into her hand. So swollen and hot, her body ached to be filled. But she didn't dare, not as aroused as she was. If he mounted her right now, she would do the forbidden and orgasm in an instant.

She licked her lips and watched him. Even bound and hanging there for her pleasure, he seemed to be the one in command of the situation. "Touch yourself," he growled in a low voice. "Show me that pretty cunt."

He thought the body she had always dismissed as scrawny and unfeminine was pretty. The thought brought a warm wave of satisfaction that mixed with her desire. After she licked one of her fingers, she slowly slid it between her smooth nether lips, parting them to reveal her clit. Hard and stiff, it poked out like a little cock. What would it feel like to have his lips wrapped around it? Would he know how to please her?

She had never been so turned on in her life.

Without preamble, she shoved her finger into her hungry pussy, gasping at the intrusion. He unconsciously rocked his hips in time with her hand, reinforcing the mental image of his cock replacing her fingers. Greedy for her orgasm, she rubbed against her clit and arched into her touch, wanting to come.

She sank her teeth into her lower lip as she tensed and added a second finger. A poor substitute for his shaft but all she could allow herself. A wave of his arousal washed through her and pushed her over the edge, her body clenching around her fingers as she hunched and cried out. Still panting and shivering, she made a low noise of frustration. The need was still there, still burning bright. Her release had taken a bit of the edge off, but she still wanted more.

Wanted *him*.

Knowing she was being stupid but unable to help herself, she pressed the release button on her bracelet and watched him roll his shoulders as the magnets holding him to his posts turned off. He tensed and took a step toward her, freezing when his collar buzzed a warning.

"Clean me," she said in a low voice. He radiated lust, which was good, but the savage fuck his gaze promised would undo her. All that male power and need focused on her; it made her feel at once helpless and powerful. In an effort to remind herself he wasn't hers, she added, "Crawl to me."

He stood there, trembling. His gaze locked on her pussy, and he began to pant. "I hate you."

"Crawl." His words hurt, and she cursed herself for being such a fool. This was only their first day of training and already she was breaking a dozen different personal rules. Barriers that had been carefully built through training and self-discipline were crumbling before a man who hated her.

He sank to his knees and slunk across the grass, his big shoulders flexing with a contained power that warmed her blood. She gave his collar a warning buzz and made him halt before her. Amusement flared in his eyes, and she had a moment to wonder if he knew her torment. Before she could tell him what to do, he moved lightning quick and buried his face between her thighs.

She intended to push his face away from her for his insolence, but she found her fingers curling in his hair instead as his broad tongue lapped at her. A rumbling purr rose from his throat and vibrated through her body. Teeth nipped at the hood of her clit, then moved away, his tongue circling around that sensitive nub of flesh but not making contact.

She tried to center herself, to regain control and instruct him on what to do. As if he needed any help. He pleasured her with a skill that left her breathless. She gripped his hair, holding him closer as he grasped her hips to keep her still for his mouth. She struggled against him, stiff beneath his hands and fighting the pleasure.

"No," she whispered and sighed as his fingers dug into her hips. The slight rasp of his stubble against her thighs brought a shiver of delight that raced down her spine. Dimly she noted his arousal increased as well. The air was thick with his pheromones, and each breath filled her body with a new rush of heat. Dangerously addictive. No wonder off-worlders were forbidden as concubines. Wars would be fought for this kind of pleasure.

A small jolt of fear cleared her head enough for her fingers to fumble to her bracelet and give him a shock. She scrambled away from him and tried to ignore the hurt look on his face as she arranged her skirts around her legs.

"Why do you run?" he asked and deliberately licked his lips.

Her hungry gaze followed the tip of his tongue, and she cleared her throat. "This isn't about my pleasure."

Sitting back on his haunches, his cock stood thick and proud from between his muscled thighs. Oh Gods, would it feel good to straddle him and ride him until they both passed out.

His lips quirked in a mean smile. "Well, it certainly isn't about my pleasure."

She lifted her chin as she smoothed the folds of her gown in a nervous gesture. Her body clamored for release, and she widened her stance to keep her thighs from rubbing together. This was going so horribly wrong. He should be the one sweating and begging right now.

DEVNAR TOOK IN a deep breath, tasting her musk and want. She had slipped back into her role as a breaker, but for a brief moment he had seen the soft woman who lay beneath all that black leather. He knew she wanted him badly. Her little pussy was terribly swollen and hot, melting into his mouth in a delicious taste that went straight to his core.

"Of course this is about your pleasure," she protested. Those unusual eyes flickered between his face and groin.

His cock throbbed with the beat of his heart, dying to be soothed by the heat of her cunt. The memory of the way she'd ground herself against his face, seeming to fight her own body's reaction, hardened him further. "If it's about my pleasure, then come over here and ride me." He stroked his hand over the head of his erection, squeezing a drop of precum and spreading it over his shaft.

The hem of her gown shivered as she crossed her arms and gripped her elbows. "You haven't earned that privilege yet."

"Really?" He stood slowly, trying not to spook her. Gaining her trust was important, the first step toward his escape. And he must escape; he must not let himself be seduced into this soft and pampered life. His men were counting on him to rescue them, and he had sworn revenge before the Goddess.

If he had to submit to her demands in order to soothe her, he would. Yeah, that was it. He was only manipulating her for his own escape. The sooner she writhed beneath him, milked his cock with her body, screamed his name, and wore his scent, the sooner he would be off this damned planet.

Even he didn't believe that lie.

He turned his wrists out so the metal cuffs gleamed in the sunlight. His shoulders dropped as he relaxed and let the heat he was feeling enter his voice. "What do I have to do to earn the right to take you? Didn't my mouth please you?"

Confusion and need flashed across her face, but her chin lifted higher. She certainly felt more comfortable in assuming the dominant role, even though he knew it wasn't what she wanted, what she needed. It might be best to let her think she had the upper hand...for the moment. "Yes, for an untrained barbarian, you did an adequate job."

He narrowed his eyes. "Adequate?" The memory of the way her body had danced beneath his mouth made him smirk.

"Yes." She tilted her little chin in a superior expression, but the nervous stroke of her bottom lip with the tip of her tongue betrayed her. Those amber streaks in her brown hair shone in the light, and her skin glowed like alabaster above the unrelieved black of her gown. He wondered if her nipples were as pink and responsive as her pussy.

He stalked toward her, and she trembled as he approached. As he stood a breath away, he again marveled that such a tiny woman could have such a big presence. She stared at him, her pupils dilating with desire. He wanted to pull her close and break through her barriers, strip her down until the passionate woman beneath all that leather begged for him.

He tried to remind himself that she was the enemy. He should punish her, make her sorry she had ever seen him. She was here to train him like a lapdog for some other cunt's pleasure. If he let her bond him, he would have to kill her. His mind rebelled at the thought, and a sharp pain punched into his heart. His instincts demanded he take care of her, soothe her obvious sexual need to make up for even thinking of harming her.

"Let's see if my hand does any better."

"Wha—"

He spun her around and pinned her arms to her sides. She struggled against him, and he groaned into the silken mass of her hair pressed against his lips. "I paid attention to what you did when you touched yourself for me." Her body softened against him, and her thrashing became more of a test of his will than his strength. Moving one hand down the front of her dress, he slipped his fingertips between the slit of the skirt and brushed his palm over the curls guarding her mound.

"No," she moaned and ground her little backside against his cock. She could have used the collar at any point to stop him, and he took her omission of this fact as her silent permission to continue.

Greedy for her, he circled her clit with one finger, spreading her moisture over her swollen labia. "But if I don't show you what I learned, then how will I ever improve?" He tapped once directly on her clit. "Oh, that's right. You said something about how you're not supposed to come with me."

"Forbidden," she whispered. A tremble shook her body, but she parted her legs for him.

Her small hands reached behind and fumbled for his cock. He considered denying her access, but he craved her touch as much as he wanted her orgasm. To force her to come when she didn't want to appealed to him on a base level. If he could force her to come, to make her do something she at once wanted and didn't want to do, he would be proving himself as her dominant. He would be the one with the power to bring her mind-blowing pleasure. It was his first taste of control after his capture, and he chased after it with a ruthless desire.

"That's it," he purred and scissored his fingers around her clit. From watching her, he knew she liked rough handling. Her body responded to him like a fine-tuned instrument, her clit poking out of its hood and begging for his touch. Goddess, she felt good, so soft and pliant.

"Please stop." She gave a breathy scream as he sank his fingers into her heat. The tissues of her inner body were swollen with need and burning hot.

"I'm here for pleasure," he reminded her with a mocking tone. "And my pleasure is for your body to clench around my fingers while you orgasm."

Her grip tightened around his cock, sending sparks of delight through his body. If she kept that up, he was going to spill himself all over her back. He added a second finger and increased his rhythm, trying to find that sweet spot in her body that would have her shattering for him.

"Do you like this?" he asked and chuckled as her body gripped him. "Oh you do. You like me being in control."

"No." Her breath hitched, and a tear hit his forearm where it pressed against her small breasts.

"Liar."

Her body shuddered, and her delicious scent intensified. His sac drew tight, and he felt himself trembling on the brink of orgasm. As the stroke of her hand increased, she arched her back, trying to take as much of his fingers into her body as she could.

He struggled to hold on, to keep from fucking her tight fist. Little groans escaped her as she squeezed and pulled on him with an expert grip that had him throwing his head back.

With a swift move, she sank before him and took him into the heat of her mouth. He buried his hands in her hair and delighted in the silky texture. She shouldn't be doing this; he should be the one making her come. She opened her throat for him and swallowed his entire length.

Now it was his turn to try to pull away, to try to fight her hungry mouth. Her skill and passion trapped him as surely as the collar around his throat. She wanted his seed, and his body was all too willing to give it to her despite the protests of his mind. She swallowed hard, and the muscles of the back of her throat massaged the head of his cock, which sent him over the edge.

With a roar, he emptied himself into her mouth in long and hard spurts. The world turned black as the strength of his orgasm tore through him. He was *bonding* with the woman at his feet. Even as the pleasure built and rebounded to new levels, he tried to fight his reaction.

Licking his still-hard cock like a sweet treat, she gave a throaty hum that reminded him of a well-fed kitten. He pulled himself from her mouth and glared down at her. As much as he could glare with his body still shuddering as hormones rushed through him, rewarding him for pleasing his mate. She stared at him with a dazed expression on her beautiful face.

"Whore," he spat out with all the anger he felt for his own weakness.

She flinched but didn't move or respond. Her pupils were huge, the blue and brown rings of her irises the thinnest sliver of color. What was wrong with her?

He took a quick step back to put some distance between them to clear his mind. The aftershocks of his release still echoed through his body, and his instinct demanded he take her again. That he fuck her over and over until she was satisfied. Instead he turned his back on her.

Her voice, at once smooth and rough, scraped over his raw nerves. "You will be fed. Then we will see if you can earn the right to take me. Get ready for a fight, Prince."

Cold and harsh, her words held none of the warmth she had displayed while being trapped in his arms. He cursed himself for his weakness and kept his back turned so she couldn't see the reaction his body had to her words. His cock swelled with anticipation, but he knew the instant she left the garden because he began to soften. He clenched his hands into tight fists as his cuffs locked together in front of him, and tried to hate her as a servant led him from the garden and back to his prison.

Chapter Five

Devnar closely examined the three closed doors before him with interest. Each was made of solid black metal and no different from the other in size or shape. As he flared his nostrils, he took a deep breath of the air and detected the musk of two unfamiliar, healthy males. The small room gave no hint as to why he was here. A sturdy bench holding a pitcher of water and three ceramic cups stood against the far wall.

The servant that had led him to the room would give him no indication of what was inside. Everyone here seemed fiercely loyal to their Mistress and unwilling to talk to him. The only time he had ever gotten a reaction was when he had called Melania a bitch in front of his groomer. The man had been massaging his back at the time, and he gripped Devnar's nerves into a cruel pinch and informed Devnar that if he ever wanted to walk without pain, he would mind his tongue about the Mistress.

Anticipation curled through his stomach and fired his muscles into movement. Melania had mentioned something about a fight. While he didn't imagine she would enter an arena with him and attempt to kick his ass, he was still intrigued. A good tussle would go a long way toward soothing his boredom. Going from training every day to being forced to lounge around had taken its toll on him mentally and physically.

He rocked back on his heels and glanced down at the thin, gold silk pants that covered his legs. He might as well be naked for as much protection as they provided. At least the boots they'd given him were serviceable. Once again the servants of this place proved to be no help in escape; they treated him more like an object than a person. Not like Melania. She seemed fascinated by him.

His thoughts took a bitter turn as he ran over their time in the garden together. So she seemed interested in his clan symbol; she didn't know that by admiring it, she had stroked his pride. What aroused him even more was knowing he clearly affected her as much as she did him. There was a vulnerability about her that intrigued him and tugged at his heart.

The door behind him opened, and Melania entered the room with two men being led on leashes. Instead of the gown from earlier, she wore the same leathers as when he first saw her. Tight and shiny, they fit every subtle curve of her slender body. On her right stood a muscular blond man with arrogant blue eyes; on her left stood a taller and leaner man with short sable hair and deep brown skin. A goatee framed the most sensual lips he had ever seen on a man. Each wore a silver version of the same pants he did. They studied him, and the blond smirked while crossing his lean, muscled arms over his bare chest.

Territorial anger demanded he pound their handsome faces into the ground. Before he could move, his collar buzzed a warning. That drew his attention to

Melania, and she casually stroked her hand down the back of the man with the goatee. Jealousy and hatred made him surge toward the other man, but pain dropped him to the ground before he made it to the man's throat.

The men's deep laughter twisted his stomach as one of them said, "Oh, he wants you badly, Mistress."

Mistress? Did these men belong to her? Were they warming her bed while she toyed with him in the garden? The thought of them mounting her, being given the gift of her orgasm that he was denied, had him pushing off the floor past the pain in order to glare at her.

"Hush," she said in her husky whisper as she minutely flinched beneath his glower. Both men immediately complied, and she crouched before him. The warmth of her body brushed over him, and he relaxed against his will. "Be easy, my pet." She stroked his cheek, and her touch soothed his body even as his mind rebelled.

"Don't touch me," he spat out and jerked his head away as the pain eased. With more effort than he would like to admit, he pulled himself to his feet and grimaced as the cuffs on his wrists pulled together and secured his hands in front of him with a metallic *snick*.

Completely ignoring him, Melania unclipped the leashes from the collars of the two men, and they walked around him in a wide circle, examining him. The blond gave him a derisive snort, and the brunet studied him with interest. He kept his gaze focused on Melania and curled his lip in a show of defiance.

"Attend," she snapped, and each man froze in place, then dropped to their knees with their hands clasped behind their back. The blond glanced at him with a disgusted expression, while the man with dark skin kept his eyes on the floor.

"Devnar, attend," she said in a low voice. His collar buzzed, and he knelt, hating her for making him submit before her. The fact that the men on either side of her were also kneeling did nothing for his anger. A hint of her arousal perfumed the air, and he found her watching him with hungry eyes. The realization that her body didn't warm until she was around him helped ease his jealousy enough to think.

"We are going to play a game." His eyes widened in interest, and her full pink lips quirked in a little smile. "Behind those three doors is a maze. The rules of this game are simple. You will each enter through your own door, and the first man to find me will enjoy the pleasure of my company."

Next to him, the other men shifted, and he saw their cocks grow as hard as his. No way he was going to let that blond bastard reach her first. He wasn't threatened by the dark-skinned man; something about him was soft and submissive. A low growl trickled out of his throat as the blond met his gaze and sneered.

"Attend," she said in a warning tone, and each man winced at the jolt of pain from their collar. "Gury, I brought you here to teach my pet about obedience. If you cannot set a better example, I will send you back to your trainer with a full report on your inability to please. I would have thought your week in labor would have cured you of your attitude."

The blond flushed, and the tendons in his forearms stood out in sharp relief as he nodded. "Yes, Mistress."

"Any questions?"

The dark-skinned man said in a soft voice, "What if there is a tie?"

Melania laughed and stroked his head. He turned his cheek into her palm and smiled at her in a peaceful manner that made Devnar growl again. "If there is a tie, Khilam, you will pleasure each other. Whoever has his release first loses. When the chime sounds, choose your door and run." Her mismatched gaze settled on him, and she added, "Be aware there are traps and puzzles in the maze that will disqualify the foolish."

Khilam looked at Devnar through lowered lashes and nodded. Devnar was thrown off his stride by the man's obvious desire for him. While he had no aversion toward laying with another man, he couldn't understand how Khilam could even notice anyone else when Melania was touching him. Didn't he see how beautiful she was? How much passion and warmth lay beyond that harsh exterior she worked so hard to project?

After giving them one last look, she left through the same door that she had entered. A trace of her musk remained, and Devnar took a deep breath, drinking her in.

"I'm going to fuck her and fill up every inch of that hot pussy with my seed," Gury said in a low voice and crossed his arms over his chest. "Even if she does look like an ugly boy, I'll still enjoy every minute of mounting her while you watch. Obviously you need to learn how a real man fucks."

When that didn't throw Devnar into a rage, Gury changed tactics. "I don't even know why you're here. A worker should never get the chance to touch a servant. Look at you; your nose is big and has been broken numerous times. Your face has no symmetry, and a scar twists your lower lip. I bet even your cock is ugly. Why royalty would want to sully their gene pool with yours is beyond me."

Devnar never had any use for idle chatter on the battlefield, and he didn't have any use for it here. The other two men were physically perfect, and he had a moment of doubt when he thought of his own battered body next to theirs. Compared to them, he looked like an ugly mongrel standing next to two purebred hunting dogs.

Khilam spoke up in a surprisingly deep voice. "They would choose him for the same reason they choose all their concubines. Too much inbreeding among the royal houses results in sterility and weak children. By breeding with their concubines, strong children are born and the perfection of our world continues." He gave Devnar an appreciative glance, the heat in his gaze obvious as it rested on his erection. "Sometimes a Master will choose a special person from the worker class as their concubine. They believe the flaws make their beauty and talents stand out even more."

Gury made a sound of disgust and stretched his arms over his head, turning his attention to the closed doors. "My Master would never accept anything but perfection for his breeding."

"You breed with men?" Devnar asked in a shocked voice.

The other men laughed, and Khilam said, "No. But some royal couples share a single concubine. We are there to provide the love and missing link that is essential for keeping the royal couple together." His gaze grew soft and distant. "To be the center of that much adoration is more than any man could ever hope for."

Gury snorted and paced before the three closed doors. "You can speak of love all you want. I can't wait until I become a real concubine so I can be free of this damn collar. I just know the perfect Mistress will choose me. A tall woman with lush curves and a soft body, fertile and round. Not some skinny little thing that's more male than I am."

Khilam shook his head and smiled at Gury. "With that attitude, you'll never get out of your training collar."

Devnar leaned against the wall and studied Khilam. "You really want that, don't you? To be a concubine?"

Khilam blinked his wide, dark eyes in confusion. "Of course."

"But why? Why would you want to be a slave to another's wishes?" Devnar shook his head and rolled his shoulders. "How could you stand losing your freedom?" He fought against the warmth that filled him at the thought of being with Melania for the rest of his life. Blaming his bonding hormones for his irrational feelings was becoming harder and harder to do.

"Stupid worker," Gury spat out and positioned himself in front of a door. "You're as ignorant as an off-worlder."

"I am—" His response was cut off by a piercing chime, and Gury sprinted through his door.

After giving Devnar a suspicious look, Khilam ran toward the door of his choice and disappeared into the darkness beyond.

Devnar tried to focus his scattered thoughts on the task ahead. Somewhere in that darkness, Melania waited for him. And he would be damned if it was Gury's seed that was going to fill her. He was going to make sure his little breaker came screaming his name as he pounded into her and showed her who she belonged to.

* * *

"Who are those novices you sent me?" Melania said into her communicator as she tried to control her anger. She paced the small room at the center of the maze, careful to avoid the traps around the bed. One misplaced step and she would find herself plunged into a pit.

Pimina sounded bored as she said, "What's wrong with them? You said you needed two men for a little game you were playing with the prince. Gury's a bit of a handful, but nothing you can't deal with. And Wental fought his way through the challenge ring to make it into Training. I thought he would be a perfect challenge for the prince."

Melania felt the floor drop from beneath her, and she had to glance down to make sure she was still standing and hadn't fallen into a trap. "There is no novice here by the name of Wental."

"What?" Pimina squawked loud enough that Melania had to pull the communicator away from her ear.

The chime of the bell sounded in the distance, and she glanced at the door leading to her room at the end of the maze. "There was some man named Khilam there instead. Goatee, dark—"

"Skin," Pimina finished with a growl. "That tricky bastard."

Sitting on the edge of the massive black silk-covered bed, Melania rubbed her face. "I take it you know him."

"Oh yes. I trained him myself two hundred years ago. He's in the service of Lord Mithrik."

"Shit," Melania whispered. Her pulse raced as she wet her dry lips. "Why is the servant of the Spymaster himself here?"

"Probably spying." Pimina ignored Melania's strangled laugh and continued. "Word of Lady Grenba's potential gift to the empress must have reached his ears. As loyal as he is to her, I'm not surprised he would inspect every potential concubine. He's actually being rather complimentary by sending in someone we would recognize."

"I mean, I knew that we would be the subject of much curiosity, but I expected some attempts to bribe the servants and workers. Not actually sending one of his men." She squared her shoulders and took a deep breath. "Well, he won't have anything to complain about when he leaves. I'll see to that."

Pimina's silence allowed her to hear a roar of male anger in the distance. "I have to go. The men will be here soon." She quickly opened the maze file on the viewing wall and directed the placement of walls so that Khilam and Devnar would arrive at around the same time.

"Don't let Lord Mithrik's pet throw you off balance."

"I won't."

Melania closed the communication link, tried to slow her pulse, and listened for any sound that might announce the appearance of one of the men. Half of her hoped it was the blond novice who found her first. She could handle him, and the jealousy might be good for Devnar. Though the way he seemed to be attracted to Khilam could definitely help. For that matter, showing Khilam what he was capable of could secure Lord Mithrik's help in making sure that the empress chose Devnar. Her heart lurched at the thought, but she tried to lock her own selfish wants and needs away. This was about his pleasure, always his.

While she chewed on her thumb, she tried to focus herself on the change in plans. This had to be handled delicately. She'd promised him her body if he won, and she had to keep that promise if she had any hope of breaking him. Most royalty put great value on their word, and she could only hope his planet was not so different.

As she watched the door, she kept imagining his big shoulders filling the frame, those dark eyes filled with hunger for her. The throb between her legs betrayed her true desires, and she longed to wrap her body around him as he thrust into her. If he won, she would send the other men away and enjoy him in private. No, Khilam had to stay if it didn't upset the prince too greatly. A cold trickle of guilt cut through her worry and accused her of arranging this just so she could see Devnar enjoying himself with Khilam.

Her long nails cut into her palms as she clenched her hands into fists. No, not her pleasure. His pleasure, always his and never hers. He was meant for the empress, and she would be able to choose her own concubine. After a lifetime of sacrifice and loneliness, she would finally have everything she wanted.

Too bad the only one she wanted was the one she couldn't have.

* * *

Devnar took a deep sniff, then moved silently around a curve in the wall and caught movement out of the corner of his eye. Gury stood at the end of a closed passage, his hands on his hips as he studied the wall in front of him. Dim light shone from the ceiling far above and gave just enough illumination for Devnar to make out a pattern on the wall that Gury examined.

From a corridor to the right, Khilam strode past with an arrogant wink at Devnar. He pressed deeper into the shadows and tried to decide what to do. Should he wait and see what Gury was up to, or should he follow Khilam?

The decision was made for him as Gury set his hands on the wall and screamed in fury. The wall flashed once, and the metallic cuffs on Gury's wrists were sealed to it. Devnar stood and took the corridor opposite of Khilam. The pitfalls of the maze were simple and easily avoided. They were nothing compared to the very real dangers of his home world.

No man-eating plants, poison flowers, or sinkholes waited for him here. Only discolored stones and nearly invisible trip wires. A faint waft of female musk tinted the air, and his body tightened with anticipation. He followed that invisible lead until he came to a set of doors, where he found Khilam leaning against them.

His skin was even darker in the low light, and his teeth flashed white as he smiled. "Excellent job."

With a low growl, Devnar crouched and launched himself at Khilam as the man shouted, "Wait, I wanted to ask—"

They both barreled through the door together and almost fell as a patch of tile dropped away, revealing a cushioned pit. Melania screeched and scrambled back on a huge bed covered in shiny black fabric. Devnar had only a moment to register her shocked expression before Khilam flipped him onto his back in a move any of his warriors would envy.

"Attend!" she screamed and sent shocks of pain through both their collars. Aroused by her musk, which permeated the room, and angered by the challenge to her body the other man presented, Devnar roared his fury at her in a cry that echoed off the walls of the small room.

Blinding pain shot through his body again, searing his nerves and helping him to regain a portion of his control. She was scared, and her fear only added to his need to defend and protect her. Next to him, Khilam did the only thing he could to possibly defuse the situation.

Fighting the pain of the collar, Khilam lay before him, exposing his belly in a submissive move. "I yield."

Devnar blinked down at him, a growl trickling out of his throat. Those two words had been burned into his mind as a trigger to step down from his rage. Thousands of hours on the practice field, all those fights and drills ending with the same words.

"I yield," Khilam repeated again.

Devnar struggled for control of his runaway rage and forced himself to take a deep breath. He briefly wondered how Khilam knew the right thing to do and say to help Devnar step back from the killing edge, but those words were as old as time and known throughout the galaxy. Khilam's glance darted between him and Melania on the bed, and a look of understanding came over his face. He made a great show of looking away from her. Devnar's temper cooled further.

Silk rustled as Melania made a move on the bed, and Khilam whispered, "Stay still."

Khilam raised himself slowly and scooted away from the bed. Devnar's sanity returned as the man backed away from Melania.

"Wait," Melania commanded.

Devnar turned to her with a snarl, but the terrified woman from moments ago was gone. The fear was still there, but it was mixed with anger now. "Khilam, prepare him for me."

"Mistress, I don't—"

"Silence," she yelled, and Devnar shuddered. His primitive brain rejoiced in her strength and power. She would make a wonderful mate and would be a fierce protector of their children. He immediately tried to dismiss the thought. She wasn't a potential mate; she was his captor. The more he tried to remind himself that she was his enemy, the more the primitive part of his brain showed him images of his babe suckling from her breast.

Goddess, he was losing his mind.

Ignorant of his internal struggle, Melania turned to him and said in a low voice, "You will let Khilam ready you for me. You are doing this for my pleasure. I want to see him touch you."

His body throbbed with her words, and all he could do was nod. The woman he was bonding with against his will wanted him to do something for her pleasure, and he was helpless to resist. The cold, cynical part of his mind wanted him to leap across the room and snap her neck before he completed the bond. His heart, his soul demanded he make her his. He would show her he was the dominant male here, the only one worthy of her regard.

He stalked over to Khilam and pressed his body into the other man's, giving him a cold smile as he felt Khilam's cock thick and hard against his stomach. For all his protests, the man wanted him, and the knowledge spurred Devnar's desire higher. Showing off in bed for a female was an art form on Jensia, and he was going to employ all his skills to make her want him more.

A small gasp from his woman wrapped around his body as he captured Khilam's mouth in a hard kiss. Using the other man's hair as a handle, he turned Khilam so she could watch them move against each other. The scent of her desire teased his sensitive palate, and he rumbled in satisfaction.

Khilam moaned into his mouth, wrapping his hands around Devnar's shoulders and sliding down his back to his ass. Still gripping a handful of his hair, Devnar guided Khilam's willing mouth down to his nipples, letting him lick and tease at the gold rings Melania had had him pierced with. The soft rasp of Khilam's tongue against the metal made Devnar's cock jump.

As Khilam's lips traveled lower, he turned to watch Melania. She stared at them, utterly rapt and panting. Her pale cheeks flushed pink as she noticed him observing her. Their gazes met for a brief moment, and the heat between them seemed to burn the air. A warm mouth licked at the hollow of his hip, and he groaned, spreading his legs in a silent invitation. The memory of how much she liked to suck his cock hardened him further.

He closed his eyes and tried to regain some form of control. The man below him delicately sucked on his sac through the thin cloth of his pants, pulling another wave of need from his body. Another mouth wrapped around the head of his shaft, and he stumbled against the twin assault.

Melania's small hands gripped his thighs, forcing him to stay in place while she licked him with low sighs and tugged his pants down to free his erection.

Khilam brushed her hair back from her cheek, and Devnar gave a warning growl at the intimate gesture. She pulled back and pressed a button on her bracelet. With a low hum, the magnets of his wrist cuffs clicked together.

"Stay still," she whispered over the sensitive skin of his hip. He struggled against the bonds, torn between the feeling of being trapped and the impossible pleasure they were offering him. All thoughts of rebellion fled his mind as she pulled Khilam's face next to hers and their tongues danced against each other and the head of his erection at the same time.

Only their hands on his thighs and ass kept him upright. He rocked his hips in a slow and lazy motion, taking satisfaction in the way they both tried to chase his cock with their mouths. Khilam began to unfasten the top of Melania's leathers, and Devnar's objections died on his lips as her small and perfect breasts came into view.

Barely enough to fill Khilam's palm, the tips burned a deep cherry color against the paleness of her skin. She arched back, offering herself to his gaze while Khilam tugged at the tips of her breasts. With one hand, Khilam tormented her nipple into a hard peak while he jerked Devnar's cock with the other.

"Suck me," he ordered in a rough voice.

With a soft laugh, Melania gathered Khilam's hair back into her fist and moved his head to Devnar's straining erection. Obediently opening his mouth, Khilam swallowed him down while Melania set the pace of his sucks. Her heavy-lidded gaze met Devnar's and she drew in a shuddering breath. Devnar could taste her passion, her need, and the sight of her stiff nipples begging for his attention drew his balls up tight to his body.

Khilam groaned, going on his hands and knees to open his throat for Devnar. He pounded into the man's mouth, sweat breaking out on his body, his gaze never leaving Melania's. Khilam's soft beard tickled his balls as he took Devnar's erection deep into his throat.

"Come for me," she said in harsh whisper. Her whole body vibrated, and she strained toward him, pulling Khilam's mouth back, then plunging down on his cock until he choked.

He jerked his hips and tore his prick from Khilam's greedy mouth. Grasping the base of his cock with his cuffed hands, he came in long, hard jets all over Khilam's face. The man closed his eyes and tipped his head back, shuddering and twitching as each splash of seed painted his cheeks and lips white.

Devnar fell to his knees as Melania moaned and licked his cum from Khilam's face with long swipes of her tongue. He panted and unconsciously strained at his bonds as Khilam made little pleading noises while she cleaned his face of every last trace of seed. Khilam's cock throbbed between his legs.

He felt a moment of pity for the other man. It wasn't like Khilam had any more say in the matter than Devnar did, less if you considered this was the only life he'd ever known. Devnar studied them as they held each other, their bodies still shuddering with the aftermath of his orgasm. With the brown silk of her hair mussed, she looked softer than he had ever seen her before. Especially framed against the dark beauty of the other man.

And Khilam was beautiful. With sharp cheekbones and a prominent jaw, his face was still masculine, but his full lips and tilted dark eyes held a hint of feminine beauty. The front of his thin silk pants strained against the outline of his erection, and Devnar's own cock twitched in response.

Melania took in a deep breath and stroked her pale hand down Khilam's broad chest, clearly displaying the other man for him. She licked her lips and subtly squeezed her thighs together. Her clever fingers played with Khilam's nipple, all the while giving off enough desire to drown him. Devnar gave her a small smile that made her eyes widen and the pulse in her neck race.

Chapter Six

Khilam looked at Devnar's groin and made a strangled sound. "He's ready to go again?"

Leather creaked as Melania crawled toward Devnar on her hands and knees. The way her leathers stretched over her bottom sent a bolt of lust straight to his balls. His cock throbbed as she licked his inner thigh, working her way up his chest.

She pressed herself against him and gave a wiggle of her hips that had him groaning. "Do you like him?"

Nuzzling the side of her neck, he licked her pulse. Her need and arousal wrapped around his senses, fueling his desire to fulfill all her needs. "The question is, do you?"

She sighed and ran her hands over his shoulders, teasing him with little pricks of her nails. "You two would look lovely together, but this is about your pleasure." The longing in her voice decided for him. He would do anything to please her, and to be honest, he wanted to sample more of what Khilam had to offer.

"I'm going to fill you full of cum," he whispered. "Then I want him to lick you clean." On his planet, it was considered a great honor to taste another man's seed in a woman's body. It was a sign of trust and friendship, as well as highly arousing to all involved. While he didn't consider Khilam a friend, he was an ally in his efforts to make his little breaker lose control.

"Gladly," Khilam said in a low rumble as he wrapped his arms wrapped around her and pressed her between them. The surge of her desire fed his own, and he found himself once again deep in the need to mate. Until she was satisfied, her desires would keep driving his own until he passed out. As their bond strengthened, he would be driven to ensure her satisfaction. This was a necessary part of his people's evolution. When a Jensian female entered her fertile period once every six years, the males bonded to her would fall into a mating frenzy, taking her over and over. Melania's arousal had a similar effect on him because of their growing bond. His body would drive him to pleasure her until she was satisfied and content.

Khilam's submissive nature allowed Devnar to relax and enjoy watching his woman curve her neck to allow Khilam's lips access. This man wasn't a threat to him. He almost evoked the same protective feelings as Melania. Shaking his head at his own foolishness, Devnar ran his hands over the silk-covered steel of the other man's body. Khilam arched into his touch, and his musky desire added another layer of flavor to the air.

"Strip her," he ordered Khilam, and Khilam quickly complied, freeing her body from the constricting leathers before tossing them out of her reach on the bed. Pale and perfect, her swollen and dark pink pussy glistened with her need. Devnar went to touch her, but his hands were still bound together.

"Release me."

She hesitated for a moment, her eyes clearing of desire. Khilam reached between her legs and pinched her labia together, forcing her clit to poke out from its hood while whispering, "Do it."

She fumbled with her wrist, and Devnar sighed as his hands were freed. Without another word, he scooped her off the floor and set her on the edge of the bed. It was the perfect height for him to fuck her while standing at the edge.

Devnar exchanged a glance with Khilam, and the men shared a wicked grin. With liquid grace, Khilam crawled up the bed and positioned himself next to her face. She glanced between them, her eyes wide and uncertain. He wanted her like that, kept off balance and needy. Idly he stroked his hand between her legs and circled her clit with his finger.

A soft moan worked out of her throat as she turned her head and reached up, pulling down Khilam's loose pants and helping him remove his clothes with eager hands. She grasped Khilam's dark erection in her fist and licked the bead of moisture from the flushed tip. Devnar held his cock with a shaking hand and ran the head between the slick lips of her cunt, coating himself in her cream. The fight to keep from plunging into her body grew worse as he watched her lick and suck Khilam's shaft with obvious need. She panted and tilted her pelvis to him, silently begging for cock.

He continued to stroke his cock and watch her suck Khilam. The sight of her swollen labia stretched over his dark shaft sent a bolt of pure lust straight to his balls. The tight muscles of Khilam's stomach bunched and hardened as he tried to pull back from her tight grip.

"I'm going to spill myself like an untrained novice," Khilam gritted out and fisted the sheets as she flicked her clever tongue on the underside of his cock. Devnar reached across her body and pulled Khilam toward him. Soft and full, Khilam's lips parted for his questing tongue, and he grasped Devnar's cock.

She leaned on her elbows, watching them as they curved into each other. Devnar fondled the other man's shaft, then fisted him, Khilam's length still slick from her mouth. She started to move, and he said in a commanding voice, "Stay."

She nodded and shivered as Khilam ran Devnar's cock over her pussy, pressing the head into her entrance and teasing her with it. Handled with such skill, Devnar found himself quickly teetering on the edge of another orgasm. He pumped into Khilam's fist, gasping as just the crown of his shaft sank in and out of her slick heat.

Khilam bit the pulse in his neck and whispered, "I can't wait for you to coat her cunt with your seed."

The rough talk shocked the orgasm out of him, and he roared as he spurted through Khilam's fingers and all over the slick lips of her pussy. Holding him still with surprising strength, Khilam rubbed the head of his cock at her entrance, the last spurts of his cum jetting into her warmth. She shook and made desperate little sounds, trying to push herself past the barrier of Khilam's fist and onto his cock.

Khilam pushed him out from between her legs and took his place, bending over with a low groan. He inhaled deeply and gave her cum-drenched pussy a long lick that had her hips surging off the bed. Still twitching with the aftershocks of his orgasm, Devnar rested his semihard cock against the smooth crack of Khilam's ass. Devnar reached around and grabbed Khilam's cock and roughly jerked him as Khilam ate the cum from her pussy.

She tried to scramble back away from Khilam's questing tongue, but he held her in place and ate at her wet folds. Low groans came from deep in Khilam's throat as he licked and sucked at the seed that had spilled down the crack of her bottom. He lifted her hips and ran his tongue over the tender pink bud of her ass.

Devnar rocked his hips against Khilam, his loose balls slapping at Khilam's ass while Devnar jerked him harder. Beneath him, Khilam tensed and shuddered, shouting his pleasure with a long groan as his hot cum coated Devnar's hand. He easily supported the other man's sagging weight, and Devnar gently lowered him to the floor.

From her scent, Melania was almost out of her mind with lust. He held up his hand to her face and shared Khilam's seed. They licked it off his fingers together, their tongues intertwining. At his feet, Khilam let out a small groan and rested his head against Devnar's thigh. His questing fingers found the loose skin of Devnar's sac, and he gently stroked him until his cock grew hard and firm.

With his hand clean, she pushed away from him and fumbled with her leathers that Khilam had tossed onto the bed. Her hands trembled, and she made a little helpless sound as he smacked her fingers away. Desperate, she tried to crawl away from him, but he hauled her back with a dark laugh.

"Not yet, Mistress," Devnar said in a mocking voice. Her eyes grew wide, and she squeaked as he dove at her. Rolling to the side, she pressed a button on her bracelet, and the cuffs on his wrists snapped back together.

The soft silk of Khilam's hair brushed his thigh as the other man ran his tongue over Devnar's sac. He stepped back and let Melania see the man working him and gave her an arrogant grin when she gasped and pressed her thighs together. He mouthed the words *Send Khilam away.*

Her back stiffened, and she gave Khilam a worried glance. Chewing on her thumb, she slid off the bed and pulled Khilam to his feet. After stroking his dark hair back from his face, she gave him a soft kiss and patted his butt.

"Go."

Khilam's eyes were dazed, and he reached for Devnar before letting his hand drop. As he gathered up his discarded pants and boots, he took in a shuddering breath. "What is he? I've never felt anything like that. Utterly addictive." The last part was said in a soft whisper, and Khilam clenched his jaw, obviously regretting having spoken the words aloud. Khilam visibly tried to regain control of himself, closing his eyes and resting his head on her shoulder.

"I said go." Her smile turned cold. "I'm sure your Master will want to hear all about your visit."

Khilam jerked back and nodded, his eyes still glazed with passion. "This has been most educational, Mistress."

Khilam walked over to Devnar and placed a soft kiss on his forehead. "You will make a wonderful concubine."

Devnar jerked out of his grip with a snarl. "Never." Was he the only one who heard the hesitation, the doubt in that one word?

Khilam laughed softly and shook his head as he quietly closed the door after him. The scent of fear spiked over her desire, and Devnar studied his little Mistress closely with a wicked smile. He had won the right to her body, and he was going to make her come even if it killed him.

HEART IN HER throat, Melania watched Devnar and tried not to let her fear show. Now that they were alone, she regretted sending Khilam away. At least when he was here, she was able to use him as a buffer between them. Now his absence only heightened her awareness of Devnar. His presence filled the room until all she could think about, all she could feel was Devnar. The scent of his sweat, the taste of his skin, his very presence seemed to invade her soul until it felt as if he were becoming a part of her.

"Why do those men think I'm something called a worker?"

His question caught her off guard, and she fumbled with the open fastenings of her leathers as she struggled to put them back on as quickly as she could. The edge of the top brushed her sensitive nipples, and she bit back a moan. "I don't know."

His laughter held a mocking edge of anger. "Don't bother lying to me, Melania." He held out his shackled wrists to her. "Release me."

This close, his scent rushed over her in a drugging wave. It relaxed her body and mind into a state of warm pleasure. "I shouldn't."

As he crouched before her, she stared at his cock as it lengthened beneath her gaze. "Please, Mistress." He leaned forward and rubbed his face against her leg. In her heightened state, the brush of his cheek had her womb clenching in need.

Fumbling with her control bracelet, she pressed the button to release his wrist cuffs and tensed in the anticipation of his touch. Much to her disappointment, he merely shook out his arms and continued to watch her. "Why am I addictive?"

She couldn't answer him, couldn't let him know how he affected her. "I don't know."

He shook his head, and she had a moment to register his disappointed expression before he was on her. With a rough jerk he pulled her leathers off her shoulders and down her arms. Before she could resist, he grabbed his discarded pants and expertly bound her hands together in a tight knot of golden silk. She couldn't even wiggle her fingers.

"What are you doing?" she said. His muscles flexed as he picked her up, and she let out a squeak when he tossed her into the middle of the bed with ease. Predatory, huge, he crawled across the black silk and loomed over her. His big fists planted on either side of her head, he leaned in and took her lips in a long and drugging kiss.

"I'm tired of you lying to me," he said in a mild voice. "So let's see if I can get some truth out of you. If you're even capable of telling the truth."

She squirmed beneath him, fear and desire mixing together in a confusing rush of heat. "You'll be punished for this."

He nodded, still straddling her. As she looked down the length of his body, she wet her lips at the sight of his thick shaft and heavy sac swaying above her. "That may be true, but right now we are alone." He tugged her leathers down around her hips so her breasts lay exposed before him. "And I plan on getting some answers from you."

She flinched as he dipped his head and took her nipple in his mouth. Instead of the painful bite she expected, his long and soft suck had her arching her hips off the bed beneath him. Pleasure burst through her body, and she moaned.

"We'll start with something simple." He pressed the tip of her nipple to the roof of his mouth and sucked hard before releasing her. "Why can't you come?"

She was surprised to find herself blushing and avoiding his gaze. "It is forbidden."

He sighed and went back to assaulting her breast with his mouth, drawing sensations out of her body she didn't know were possible. "We already went over that. Why is it forbidden?"

She pressed her lips together, and he leaned forward, teasing them apart with his tongue. "Why?"

"Because you aren't mine." Her breath came out in a soft sob. "Because you will belong to the empress, and I cannot have you. I'm so alone, and I cannot have you."

He froze above her, and to her shame, she felt tears welling in her eyes. Rough hands ran down her arms and over the sides of her ribs, awakening her skin to his touch.

He bent to lick her belly button, gently nipping the soft skin. "Why am I addictive?"

She gripped the sheets above her head, trying to force her body to be still beneath his sensual assault. "Your hormones," she hissed as he drew her boots off and pulled her leathers down her body. The cool air hit her skin but did nothing to dampen the heat. He felt so good above her, and they both sighed as he laid his body flush against hers.

"My hormones," he prompted and nudged at the entrance to her pussy with the head of his cock.

"When you come, you release…" Thinking about anything but the sensation of the velvet head of his shaft pushing into her became unimportant.

He pulled back and moved his hand between them, wetting his fingers in her cream and spreading it over her clit with a butterfly-soft touch. "Tell me, Melania."

The way he said her name had her rolling her hips toward him. "Your hormones, they are like a drug to us. Your release feels so…amazing. Even the taste of your seed makes my mind flood with pleasure."

"Interesting." He wrapped a fist into her hair and forced her gaze to his. "I want you to watch me while I take you."

Her mind tried to tell her to stop, that this was horribly wrong, but she lay helpless beneath him. Ever so slowly, he slid his thick cock into her, rubbing against the swollen inner walls of her body. It was beyond anything she had every felt, so good it shook her to her soul.

"Goddess, you're so tight," he whispered, then fought to push his way into her body. At last he was all the way in, and she writhed beneath him. So full, he fit her like the missing piece of her body. The head of his cock dragged inside her as he pulled back, and she screamed.

"Like that?" His deep laugh at once filled her with shame at her lack of control and desire. "Answer me."

"Yes," she whispered and tried to draw him back in.

He looped her bound hands behind his neck and buried himself inside her with a painful thrust that had her arching against him. "Such a hot little cunt, and so wet for me."

She snapped her hips to meet his as their rhythm increased. She needed this, needed his cock, needed him fucking her. Their bodies rubbed against each other, and his rising hormones began to work her into a frenzy. Whimpering, she kissed the side of his neck, his chin, silently begging him for more.

"Melania, come for me." That command, said by her a thousand times to novices, had its intended effect.

He pinned her hips to the bed and ground his pelvis into her, his cock swelling while he pressed on her clit. With a loud scream, she shattered around him and began to orgasm. Heat, pleasure, and fear overwhelmed her as he held her. Her body gripped his, trying to milk the thick and hard cock that still throbbed inside her. Slowly the pleasure pulled back, and her body hummed with the energy of her release.

Even as a pleasure greater than anything she had ever known crested inside her, guilt mixed with despair tried to rush into its place. How could she disobey everything she had worked for, everything she had ever been taught, all for the sake of a fleeting moment's pleasure?

Devnar brushed his hand over her cheek, and it wasn't until he murmured something that she realized she was crying. On the heels of her despair, a vast relief flooded into her soul and chased the guilt away. She swore she could feel Devnar inside her, not just physically but also emotionally. It was as if she could reach into her soul, and he would be there waiting for her, a solid presence that warmed her empty heart.

Confused by her feelings, she tried to blame it on the hormones. Maybe Devnar wasn't just physically addictive to her, but also emotionally. Was it even possible to become addicted to emotion? As the warmth expanded inside her heart, touching parts of her that had ached for tenderness and love, she knew the answer was yes. She would do anything for these feelings to continue, and for that reason, she should get him away from her as quickly as possible before it became too late and she doomed them both.

She didn't resist as he removed her arms from around his neck and rolled them over. He draped her over him like a blanket and held her as she cried. When her sobs petered down to sniffles, he slowly rocked his hips where they were still connected. "Good girl," he whispered and smoothed his hands down her back.

"This is so wrong," she said in a choked voice.

He didn't respond, instead driving his cock into her with short jabs. "Ride me."

Blinking at him, she groaned when he placed her bound hands on his chest.

"Concubine, ride me." Concubine. He had called her his most beloved. True, he probably had no idea what those words meant to her, how often she had dreamed of someone as magnificent as Devnar saying them, but they still sent an erotic thrill straight to her core. She should climb off him right now and contact Pimina.

"You like that, don't you?" His intense eyes studied her face as she rocked her hips into his.

As she bit her lower lip, she nodded and sighed as his clever fingers found her nipples.

DEVNAR ROLLED HER swollen tips between his fingers, groaning as her tight little body clamped around his. She was so beautiful. Her skin shone like a pearl against his. The flush of her hard nipples had deepened to a rose color from his rough play, and he lifted her almost all the way off his cock, watching her pussy stretch around him.

Tears still wet her cheeks, and they tugged at his heart. He tried to steel himself against the part of him that wanted to do whatever it took to make her happy. To kiss away her tears and assure her she would never have to be alone again. He drove himself into her body, delighting in how responsive she was to his every move.

She arched her back while she rode him, her little breasts thrusting into the air and begging for his hands. Her eyes closed, and her lips went slack. He felt her hesitate, draw back, and try to keep herself from coming.

That was so not going to happen.

Using his strength, he pulled her forward so her clit ground against his pelvis and his cock stroked over the spot inside her pussy that made her wince. He hunched forward and ate the cries from her mouth as she began to spasm around his cock.

Heat like nothing he had ever known gripped him, and the pressure of her inner muscles jerked the orgasm from him. The jerks of his cock were almost painful as he filled her with his cum, her body milking every ounce he had to offer. She moaned against his neck, her bound hands trapped between them. Every twitch of her body drew an answering wave of pleasure from his until they both lay there shivering.

He gently untied her hands and pulled her back onto his chest before rolling them to their side. Her muffled sobs tore at his heart, and he tried to suppress the feeling of guilt that tore through the pleasure of mating with his woman. Gently stroking her hair, he placed a kiss on her forehead.

"Don't," she said weakly and pushed at his chest.

He cupped her small bottom and kneaded the tight muscles. She relaxed slightly against him, and he leaned on his elbow, looking down at her. Red rimmed her eyes, and her lips were flushed and swollen from his kisses.

"Melania," he sighed and kissed a tear from her cheek. "Was it that bad?"

Her lips quivered, and she let out a watery laugh. "No, you'll make the empress very happy."

The rejection in her words stung him, and he pulled back from her. "I don't want the empress. I want you."

Cupping his face in her hand, she studied him, and the pain in her gaze tore at his heart. "You still don't understand. I could never keep you as mine. To even think of such a thing is treason." She buried her face against his chest and took in a deep breath. "To be the concubine of the empress is more than anyone could ever hope for. You will be one of the most powerful men on Kyrimia, and your child will rule this world."

"I don't want her. I want you," he repeated. Joy flared in her eyes, and he pulled the rumpled sheet over them. "Help me escape. I'll take you with me." Startled, he realized he meant it. His plans for revenge took second place to his need to have her with him. He closed his eyes and pulled in a deep breath of her scent. His emotions alternated between joy at finding his mate and despair at his body's horrible timing. Of all the women in the universe, it had to be her, and it had to be now. Somewhere, his Goddess was surely laughing at him. He opened his eyes and held her gaze, trying to convey his sincerity. "We'll escape together, and I'll find a way to get us back to my world."

That joy in her eyes vanished as if it had never been. "Are you insane?" She scooted away from him and picked her leathers off the floor with a trembling hand. "You would be caught and put to death, and I will never have my concubine—" Turning pale, she stepped into her leathers and quickly zipped them.

"You would never have your what?" He leaned forward and captured her wrist.

She jerked away from him, and a cold mask slid into place, hiding the warm and passionate woman he had just held in his arms. "Nothing."

"Melania," he said in a low voice.

She took a deep breath and slipped on her boots. "If the empress chooses you, I will be given a concubine of my own."

"Be my concubine," he blurted out before he could stop himself.

She sagged against the bed, and the pain rolled off her in a physical wave. "Don't even think such a thing."

Her words struck him like a blow, and he felt physically sick at the thought of her with another man. His heart already believed she was his, even if they hadn't completed the final step of a true bond. To have her reject him outright hurt soul-deep. But what did he expect? It wasn't like she cared about him at all. In fact, if it wasn't for his irrational bonding urges, he would have escaped long ago.

The silence stretched out between them. He longed to hurt her as much as she'd hurt him. Her rejection on top of being held prisoner brought his rage to a boiling point. "Forget I ever said anything. As if I would want such a cold and cruel bitch to be my mate." Even as he said the words, his heart constricted in pain at hurting her.

Her face paled until dark circles stood out underneath her eyes. "I—"

Even as his heart broke, the anger he had kept bottled up refused to be stopped. "You what? You and your people have no honor. All you care about is sucking me dry of every ounce of pleasure I can give you to feed your addiction."

Clutching her chest, her lips trembled as she said, "You're wrong. I'm trying to do what's best for you."

"Who gave you the right to decide what's best for me?" He turned his back on her, unable to face her pain. "Did Lord Adsel pay you off as well? Did he tell you what to do to make me bond with you?"

Confusion flashed across her face so quickly he wasn't sure he even saw it. "I have no idea what you're talking about. You're being very irrational, and I think you need to rest."

He took a step toward her, then froze when his collar buzzed. For a moment, her expression softened, but whatever she was about to say was cut off by the loud chime of a bell. She glanced at her bracelet, and her face paled at whatever she saw there.

Chapter Seven

"Devnar, attend." Her voice was as cold as he had ever heard.

He crossed his arms in a display of defiance he knew was useless. Pain lanced through him and brought him to his knees. His head roughly jerked as she fisted her hand in his hair and tilted his face toward hers. How he wished to reverse their positions, to be the one demanding obedience.

"I don't care if you hate me, I don't care what you think about me, but I will not allow you to sabotage your chances with the empress." The chime sounded again, and her lips tightened. Behind her cold mask, he saw bright and shiny fear in her eyes. "Lady Grenba is calling, and you will be a polite and dutiful slave at my feet when I answer." Her grip tightened until sparks of pain shot from his scalp. "If you're not, she will take you away and give you to another breaker."

He growled at her but nodded and gripped his hands together as his wrist cuffs snapped with a metallic click. As angry as he was at her, the thought of being handed over to the bitch who had been part of his capture made him sick.

Quickly fastening her leathers, she brushed her bracelet and the far wall turned opaque, then filled with the image of Lady Grenba. Dressed today in a shimmering ivory velvet gown that highlighted her deep brown skin, she idly stroked the hair of a bald and chained man kneeling at her feet. A wave of bile surged in his stomach as he saw the cruel metal device attached to the man's testicles. An elaborate cage with little golden weights stretched the skin of his sac until it was almost tissue thin. Despite his obvious discomfort, the man sported an impressive erection.

"Lady Grenba, how may I serve?" Melania kept her voice carefully neutral, but her hand in his hair loosened its grip, and she stroked him gently.

"Breaker," Lady Grenba said with a sneer. "I'm checking on my property. How goes his training?"

"Very well, your ladyship."

Lady Grenba examined him closely from the screen, and he had to lower his head to hide his disgust. "Ready him for public display."

Next to him, Melania tensed and shifted so she stood in front of him, partially blocking his view of the screen. "Your ladyship, I don't think he is—"

"I didn't ask you what you thought, Breaker." The man at Lady Grenba's feet shivered at her tone, and the weights on his testicles clanked together. "He had better outshine every novice there, or I will give him to a breaker who knows how to serve."

"Yes, your ladyship." Though the words were perfectly bland, Devnar watched Lady Grenba's eyes narrow with anger as Melania stepped slightly in front of him so that her bottom pressed against his shoulder, but he could still see the screen Her slender frame had no hope of blocking him, but she was definitely trying to shield him. On the screen, the lines around Lady Grenba's mouth deepened as her lips twisted into a snarl.

"You think you can protect him from me?" Lady Grenba rose from her chair and moved toward the screen until her green eyes filled it, blazing with anger.

"No, your ladyship." Despite her words, she didn't move from in front of him. Part of him was appalled his woman was putting herself in danger for him, and the other part took her defense as a sign of her caring.

Lady Grenba's voice dropped to a croon. "Do you think to shield him from me? Do you wish he was yours to fuck and cuddle?" Melania didn't answer, and she continued with a cruel smile. "You do, don't you?" Laughing, Lady Grenba clapped her hands with delight. "Oh how delicious!"

A tremor ran through Melania's body, and he gently pressed his shoulder to the back of her thigh. It was all he could do to comfort her, but he couldn't let her suffer like this. Her shaking stilled, and she traced the tips of her fingers over his forehead.

"Bring him to the Volsun Arena tomorrow morning. The empress will be there to watch the fights, and it will be the perfect opportunity to whet her appetite for the prince." Lady Grenba used the tip of her slipper to nudge at the cage on the man's testicles, jerking a groan of pain from him as he fought to keep still. "Are you enjoying him, Breaker?" The question was said in an idle tone of voice while she toyed with her slave, but even Devnar didn't miss the undertone of laughter.

Melania's hand stroked over his cheek and the tips of her nails rasped over his stubble. "My pleasure is of no consequence. I live to serve."

"Mhmm, yes. You would do well to remember that. I would hate to see one of our favorite breakers servicing every worker with a silver coin to buy her cunt." As she said this, Lady Grenba watched him and smirked as he snarled at her.

Pain from his collar sliced through his body as Melania pushed him to the floor with her boot, then shouted, "How dare you!"

He trembled with the effort to keep from screaming. Lady Grenba's cruel laughter floated through the room. "You will present yourself to Pimina for punishment after the arena, Breaker. Perhaps that will inspire you to keep your slave under better control. If he fails at attracting the attention of the empress, you will return him to me." Devnar rolled his eyes to the screen but held his tongue. Melania looked as if she might come apart, and he couldn't save her if she did.

Melania's reply might as well have been a scream for all the anger in her words. "Yes, your ladyship."

The man at Lady Grenba's feet let out a long scream like a trapped rabbit as Lady Grenba leaned over him. His face was lost in the sweep of her black hair as she kissed him, and Melania tried to shield his eyes from the screen. Before it blanked out, Lady Grenba raised her face to them with a hideous smile and spat out pieces of the male slave's lips. His high screams echoed after the picture went blank.

Devnar pushed himself to his knees with a groan and braced himself with one hand against the floor. Trying to gather his scattered thoughts, he felt the anger from earlier drain away as the screen went opaque and the chime sounded again. Bile rose in his throat, and he wanted with all his heart to hold Melania, to promise her he would kill their enemies and keep her safe. Lady Grenba would fit right in with the slave raiders of his planet. Hell, as sadistic as she was, she'd probably end up their queen.

Melania stared down at him, her lips pressed into a thin line. He tried to find the words to apologize, but she shook her head and placed her hand over his mouth. "This is my fault. I pampered you too much and forgot my duty. If you don't capture the empress's attention, I know what Lady Grenba will do to you, and I wouldn't wish that on my worst enemy. I will do anything to keep you from her." One tear spilled down her cheek, and she gave him a sad smile. "After the arena, I will ask that you be assigned to another breaker. I'm sorry I failed you, my prince."

He tried to grasp her, but she darted away and ran out the door before he could move. She couldn't leave him; the very thought drove a wedge of despair into his stomach. He tried to tell himself he only cared because she was his link to escape, and his stunned mind tried to think of a way to salvage this situation. The door slid open, and an older woman dressed in a long gray gown snapped her fingers. He didn't resist when, with a disapproving frown, she motioned for him to follow her.

Steam billowed from the open doorway of the groomers, and the woman stopped him from entering with a finger pointed into his chest. "I don't know what you did to the Mistress, but she is sobbing her heart out right now. You should be ashamed."

Devnar gaped at her and managed to say, "I should be ashamed? She's the one keeping me here against my will, forcing me to do"—he hesitated and actually blushed as the old woman raised her eyebrows—"things that I don't want to do."

The maid glanced down the hallway behind her, then lowered her voice, "Do you have any idea how lucky you are that you got her as a breaker? She is far too kindhearted for an off-world barbarian like yourself. We've heard about you people, raping and pillaging your way through the galaxy, abducting women, and treating them worse than the lowest whore." She raised her hand against his face and shook her finger at him when he tried to interrupt her. "Most breakers would have tortured you into submission long ago, but the Mistress always tries to use pleasure instead of pain. Almost every person in this household has been saved from an abusive owner by the Mistress, and I won't have a fool you—"

He was getting really tired of women calling him a fool. Crowding into her personal space, he backed her against the wall and growled down at her. "What business is it of yours what happens between us, servant?"

She grasped her hands in the front and tried to stare him down. "We know that if she manages to make you into something suitable for the empress"—the disbelief in her words made him snort—"she will have a chance to have a concubine of her own. She deserves the chance at happiness fate took from her when it cursed her with those eyes."

"I want her to be *my* concubine. I want to make her happy." He tried to gesture with his hands, forgetting they were bound. Behind her, his skinny groomer wandered into the doorway and watched him with narrowed eyes.

The maid's shoulders dropped, and she shook her head. "You really don't understand anything about us, do you? Having a concubine is her only chance at ever having a child and a family of her own to love. She can't have a child with you. We are all sterilized at birth. That's the way it has to be so we don't repeat the overpopulation that helped destroy our planet tens of thousands of years ago. Only the empress can grant us the right to bear children. The Mistress can't even marry for fear of passing on her birth defects."

Devnar gaped at her in shock. "What are you talking about, her birth defects? Melania—the Mistress is perfect. So she has two different-colored eyes, who cares? Her heart and soul are as strong as any warrior's."

The maid gave him a considering look before carefully saying, "Novice, it is not just her eyes. Her body did not develop like a proper woman's. She has no curves and lacks the height that our people prize in their females. Every single birth is carefully planned so we only pass on the best possible chances at survival to our next generation. The Mistress is considered rather ugly by our standards of attractiveness, however beautiful her heart and soul are. That's why she was given up at birth."

The ache in Devnar's head deepened as he tried to wrap his mind around what the maid was saying. Being forbidden to marry, to have the love of a mate and family struck him as horrific. And for someone as naturally caring and loving as Melania, it must have been hell on earth. "Wait, if having a child is such a privilege, why did her parents give her away?"

The man that served Devnar as his groom stepped out of the doorway leading to the baths. "They didn't really have a choice. Her cursed eyes slated her for life as a whore in a worker's brothel from the moment it became apparent they were flawed. By giving Melania up to the regulators to be used as a servant, her parents were given permission to have another child, one they could hopefully keep."

His words hit Devnar like a blow. "That's atrocious."

The maid lifted her nose and gave him a cold stare. "That's reality, Novice. Didn't you ever wonder why being a concubine is such an honor? It is one of the few ways anyone from the servant class can be assured the chance to have a child. Otherwise it's a random lottery, with a one in a hundred chance that you'll be picked if you have the right genetics." Her hands fluttered before her as she spoke. "We are a long-lived people; three hundred years is not unheard of. Can you imagine how many children one pair of people could have in three hundred years? What livable space we have would be gone, and we would destroy the planet a second time and finish our race off for sure."

Devnar's groom crossed his skinny arms. "And for someone with the Mistress's abnormalities, having the empress accept you as a concubine will be the only chance she will ever have to bear a child."

She searched his face with a pleading expression. "It is known you belong to Lady Grenba. If the Mistress fails with you, the lady will punish her in ways you cannot imagine."

His stomach clenched into a hard knot at the memory of the blood dripping down Lady Grenba's teeth and onto her cream gown. He backed away from the maid hovering in the doorway of the groomers. On the other side, his groomer leaned against the frame, clearly blocking his entry.

The groom nodded toward the serving woman and said in a low voice, "Show him, Salina."

Flushing, she fiddled with the laces at the front of her dress and began to unlace her top. "I don't think it's necessary—"

The lean man slowly shook his head. "He won't understand what will happen to the Mistress until you show him." The groom placed his hands on Devnar's shoulders and turned him to face the maid. Not meeting his eyes, she finished unlacing her dress and pulled it down over her shoulders. Where her breasts should have been were scarred lumps of tissue, twisted into misshapen mounds. Devnar tried to step back, but the man held him.

The groom's voice sounded from over his shoulder. "Salina used to belong to Lady Grenba. She put herself between the lady and a man she was torturing. Salina was fond of him, and the lady, drunk and careless, was about to kill him. To pay for interrupting her pleasure, Lady Grenba had Salina's breasts burned off."

"My husband, Danilel, loved my breasts. He said they were the one place on earth he felt safe," Salina said softly. "And Lady Grenba was always jealous of them. Always looking for an excuse to cane me in front of her troops, to tie them in complex knotted ropes until they turned purple with lack of circulation. She had her men do things, horrible things to me while she watched. I—" Her voice cut off in a thick choke.

A nauseous heat broke out over his body as he watched her lace her dress back in place. He slumped against the wall and wiped the oily sweat from his forehead. The faces of Melania and his sister flashed before him, each being put through the torture Salina had described. "No more, woman. I'll think about what you said."

He looked up, then reached toward her, hesitating when she pulled away. Patiently he waited with his hand held out. Just a little trust was needed. He let the tension flow out of his body and assumed the stance he often had to use with his sister when nightmares came over her. Using the hard-won patience he had learned, he stood as still as he could. To Salina, he was a man, and men meant pain. The switch came over Salina's eyes, and she placed her wrist in his hand.

"Thank you for the honor of showing me your battle scars."

The old woman tugged at her hand and blushed. "They aren't—"

"Yes, they are. You went to war for the most noble of intentions, keeping your friend alive. All other goals fall into ashes before it. In a war of purity versus evil, the darkness will always fall, and justice will always find a way." He knelt before her and kissed her hand. "You honor me, lady, with your tale."

Unshed tears gleamed in her eyes as she took a deep breath. "Maybe you aren't quite the barbarian we were led to believe." She looked at the groom, and he nodded. "Lady Grenba's servants made sure we knew you broke a trainer's arm. You have to understand why we feared for our Mistress around you."

"They gave me *trunage*." Devnar ignored their gasps at the mention of the powerful aphrodisiac. "I wouldn't whore for them, so they gave me enough of it that I lost my mind. I guess my body chemistry reacts differently. Instead of putting me into a mating rut, it put me into a battle frenzy."

Salina opened her mouth, but the groom cut her off. "Let it be." She nodded and gave Devnar one more searching look before turning away and hurrying down the hall.

With a sharp tug on his arm, the groom led him into the white stone baths. The humid air held the mellow scent of herbs mixed with soap, and Devnar took a deep breath to cleanse his lungs. Neither man spoke as Devnar allowed the groom to gently push him into a deep pool, flinching only when the rough bristles of a brush scrubbed at his back.

"Stand," the groom said in a rough voice.

"How do you know so much about me?" He raised his bound hands above his head as the groom efficiently scrubbed his chest and stomach.

Rubbing the brush against a bar of sage soap, the groom shrugged and gestured for Devnar to raise his leg. "People talk; other people listen."

Devnar thought of how the maids at home would chatter away like excited birds whenever they got together. "If overpopulation is such an issue, why don't your people leave this planet and go live elsewhere?"

The groom gave him a hard look and rinsed the brush in the water while Devnar sank back in up to his shoulders. "The survival of our people was bought with the blood and sweat of generations. I will not dishonor my ancestors by throwing it all away for my own selfish needs. Besides, there is no law or safety outside of the domes. Only poisonous air, killing radiation, and barren land."

Devnar leaned forward as the man gathered his hair and began to wash it. "From what I saw from the ship that brought me here, your polar ice caps are reforming. There should be a decent amount of land available in a couple hundred years after all that ice pulls back the lakes and oceans. I wouldn't be surprised if there are new tracts of usable land even now."

"Lies," the groom replied in a rough voice. "The empress would have told us if there was any new land."

Sensing he had pushed the groom as far as he could on that subject, he switched tactics. "What about going to another planet? Surely you're aware that there are thousands of worlds where you and your family could live out your days in freedom. My planet, Jensia, is always looking for honorable men."

The groom snorted. "You can't fool me, off-worlder. I know all about what waits for us on other planets. War, famine, plague, and raiders like yourself that steal our women. There isn't another planet out there that could rival the purity or security of Kyrimia. Besides, once you leave, you can never, ever come back."

The man poured a bucket of cold water over his head to rinse, and Devnar wiped the water from his eyes. He had hoped the man would express interest in getting off the planet, and then he could have used him as an ally to escape with Melania. "What about having a family of your own? Don't you want that?"

The groom unfolded a large towel, then gestured for him to step from the bath. "As long as I continue to serve with loyalty and devotion to my Mistress and the empress, there is always a chance my wife and I will be blessed. And if the Mistress were to have a child, that baby would be as much ours to love as hers."

Devnar grabbed the towel and finished drying himself. He heard the note of hesitation in the groom's voice and decided to try to dig deeper. "Really? I can't imagine if I had a wife, she would feel the same way. A child of her own to cuddle and hold or the child of someone whose house she cleans."

"Get on the table," the man said in a gruff voice.

Devnar reclined on his stomach and tried to keep his tone light as the man massaged sandalwood-scented oil into his back. He willed his body to relax, but his entire focus was on the man working his shoulders. "On my planet, a man's greatest pride and joy is his children. We value them and our mate above all else. But I guess your fear of the unknown is greater than your desire to make your wife a mother."

"And your uncontrolled rutting is the reason you have to rob from others to feed your brood. Your arrogance is appalling. Tell me this, who is loved more? The child squeezed out and forgotten among his horde of siblings, or the child waited for, prayed for, and wanted with all your heart." The man pushed away from the table and stalked toward the exit before Devnar could respond. Well, there went the idea of getting the groom to help him.

Devnar swung his feet over the side of the table and sat up as the door closed behind the groom with a pneumatic *hiss*. He tried to focus his mind on escaping, to look for an exit or something in here he could use for a weapon. Unfortunately his thoughts couldn't get past Melania's rejection and the reason for it. He couldn't really blame her for the way she had reacted. She'd been raised pretty much since birth to believe the system that had been her mother and father was all powerful and all knowing. Add to that the only love and praise she'd received probably came from doing exactly what she was told, and you had a woman who would not only be terrified of breaking the rules but conditioned to believe she wasn't worth loving.

He had to find a way to prove to her she couldn't live without him and that his feelings for her weren't just a ploy. That he could offer her things no one else in the entire universe could. If he could complete the bonding with an exchange of blood, she would be bonded to him as well. Once that emotional and spiritual link was established, there would be no way for her to hide her heart from him or protect herself from his love.

Shame rushed through him at the thought of bonding a woman against her will. It went against everything he had been taught. A bonding should only happen after both parties had agreed and spent a considerable amount of time in proper courtship. If the woman was already bonded to another male, then he would have had to court her mate just as thoroughly as he courted her. If they both accepted him, an unbreakable chain would form between their souls forever.

Not something even the most foolhardy male jumped into, but here he was, doing just that. He would have worried he'd lost his mind if not for the unshakable conviction that Melania was meant for him. It could not have been more obvious she was his destiny than if his Goddess had appeared and told him herself. He knew with every drop of blood in his body, with every breath he took, that Melania was his mate. To him it was as apparent as the sun in the sky and the ground beneath his feet. There could be no other now that he'd found her. A peace came over his soul as he realized that maybe this was the reason he had been brought here. His Goddess took an active role in the lives of her people, and it was not unheard of for her to subtly guide her worshippers to where they would be needed most.

And Melania needed him almost as much as he needed her.

A full bonding was the only solution, and he had to do it quickly. The more she cared for him, the harder she pushed him away. It was the only way to get past the walls she and her society had built around her heart.

Oh, he understood why she had those defenses. She loved to please, and it would have been impossible for her not to fall in love with every novice and concubine that came her way without enormous self-discipline. A warm glow of satisfaction filled him as he remembered the way she gave up control, how she gave him the gift of her little body tightening around him with her orgasm. That victory thrilled him as deeply as any triumph on the battlefield.

Maybe he had to look at this like a military campaign. Obviously his efforts to try to understand her on her terms had failed. If he put her actions and thoughts into the context of an enemy to be defeated, he could use all the stealth and skills he had learned in his lifetime of holding his land against the southern rebels. Her defenses were strong but not impossible to breach.

He pushed off the table and paced the small room. He would need to get her alone, someplace where she felt secure. Right now she was probably as off balance as she ever would be and was busy trying to rebuild her emotional defenses. He needed to launch his next attack before she had time to fortify her excuses and convince herself she didn't want him.

The door slid open, and Salina appeared with an armful of clothing. Putting a contrite expression on his face, he turned on the charm that never failed to get him what he wanted. He looked at the older woman through his lowered lashes and said in a soft voice, "Salina, I need to apologize to the Mistress. You're right. I feel horrible about causing her pain. I need to make amends, please," he added with a seductive rumble to his voice and hid his smile as Salina flushed and patted her gray hair.

Chapter Eight

Cekina, a pretty new maid with Melania's household, stood at the arched doorway to her bathroom and watched Melania. Lush and full figured, the dark-haired maid never lacked male interest everywhere she went. With a quiet personality and a shy demeanor, the maid was just beginning to open up to Melania.

Melania glanced at her in the mirror as she scrubbed her face with an icy washcloth. "Leave the tea on the sitting table."

"Mistress, your novice is here requesting an audience with you." A look of fear flashed across the maid's face, gone too quickly for Melania to be sure it was ever there.

With a tired sigh, Melania dabbed some cooling gel on her swollen eyelids. "I'm not in the mood." The words sounded petulant even to her, and her grimace deepened.

The maid fidgeted and cleared her throat. "Ah, I'm afraid he's already here."

Melania clutched the front of her worn periwinkle blue robe as it gaped open. "What is he doing here?" she said in an angry whisper and glanced over the maid's shoulder. Sure enough, Devnar examined a pastel painting on the wall of her bedroom. Dressed in a pair of loose black pants and a plain white shirt, he rubbed a thick scar on his jaw when he caught her staring at him. A gleam lit his dark eyes, and her body responded with a sudden surge of heat. His nostrils flared as he took in a deep breath, and the corners of his lips lifted in a small smile.

"Salina brought him, Mistress." Cekina turned and gave Devnar a quick look of approval before returning her gaze to the floor with a pretty blush flushing her cheeks. Jealousy and insecurity tightened Melania's stomach into a hard knot, and she hunched her shoulders.

Keeping her voice as calm as possible, she rinsed the washcloth out with shaking hands. "Always check with me before you admit anyone to my rooms."

"My apologizes, Mistress. Would you like me beaten?" The eagerness in Cekina's voice turned Melania's stomach. Taken from an abusive Master, Cekina still craved the beatings she associated with love. Nothing Melania had done could break the deep-seated association.

Turned from her own despair by the need to serve, Melania studied the maid. "As I've told you before, I do not beat my servants."

Anger and despair flashed through the maid's eyes before she lowered her gaze to the floor. "Yes, Mistress."

"Go and tell the staff I'm not to be disturbed for the rest of the night. I will be dealing with my novice."

Cekina fisted her hands in her skirt and hesitated, clearly contemplating doing something to earn punishment. Melania decided to take the option away from her with a direct order. "Go."

With a quick curtsy, the maid left with a sway to her hips that made Melania grit her teeth. She scolded herself for letting Cekina get to her like this. Tales had reached her ears of Cekina picking fights with the other servants and then barely fighting back when they beat on her. It wasn't fair to her staff that she kept the woman around in hopes of rehabilitating her. Cekina had needs that were never going to be met here.

Tomorrow she would have to contact Pimina and see about her getting reassigned. A little voice in her mind whispered about needing to get Devnar reassigned as well, but she ignored it. She could feel him standing in the other room, and could taste a hint of his musk and hormones in the air. Already her body craved the chemicals he gave off, and her core clenched in anticipation. Hands resting on the cool marble of her sink, she watched his back in the mirror. It still thrilled and confused her that she called forth desire from his body. That he wanted *her*.

Tossing the ice-cold washcloth into the sink, Melania tied back the tangled knot of her hair and examined her reflection. Pink blotches still covered her face, and her eyes were red and swollen. She would never be one of those women who looked beautiful when she cried. As she cleaned out her hairbrush, she delayed facing him. If there was a secret escape in her bathroom, she would have used it.

Dangerous, he was so dangerous to her hard-won self-control. The situation was spiraling out of her hands, and she felt helpless to stop it. Any option she looked at had either her alone and spending the rest of her life watching Devnar love another woman, or her dead and Devnar a tortured shadow of himself suffering for an eternity beneath Lady Grenba's bloodlust.

Since the moment he'd told her that he wanted her as his concubine, she couldn't stop thinking about his words. He couldn't know he had paid her the ultimate compliment, but that didn't stop her heart from aching every time she imagined spending the rest of her life serving him, loving him, and being loved in return. If the regulators knew she was even dreaming of such a thing, she would be publicly whipped and stripped of her breaker status.

"What do you want, Prince?" She tried to keep her tone cold and formal, but a hint of sadness peeked through. All she had thought about over the past hours was the hurt on Devnar's face, the impossible dream he had planted in her head.

"I wanted to tell you that I'm sorry."

She brushed past him and poured herself a steaming cup of tea from the tray in the small seating area. The steam curled from the delicate white cup as she stared at the amber liquid inside. "You have nothing to be sorry about. You performed well, and I have every confidence you will attract the empress's eye tomorrow."

The soft brush of bare feet on carpet made her aware of his movements a moment before his warmth brushed against her back. Instead of embracing her like she feared—wanted—he held the cup to her lips and gave her a drink. After taking a swallow of the bitter tea, she clutched the front of her robe while he set the cup back down. Now he would take her in his arms, and she would have to punish him. Punish herself.

Once again he surprised her, taking a seat in the large cream leather chair next to the small table. Utterly relaxed, he leaned forward and tugged the edge of her robe until she was standing between his legs. Such a big man, even seated he seemed to fill the room with his presence.

"Take off your robe," he ordered, and she tried to pull away.

"It's time for you to go." Her struggles were less than enthusiastic, and his laughter at once shamed and aroused her. Damn him.

"Take off your robe, Mistress." The front of his shirt gaped open, showing a square of firm chest and the corded muscles of his throat as he leaned forward. Holding her gaze, he gave the belt holding the fabric in place a gentle tug.

Anger filled her and blended with her rising passion. It was impossible to think around this man, to keep her mind and body from hungering for him. Her hand moved to touch her bracelet controlling his collar, and he made a low growl.

"I wouldn't do that if I were you." His voice was low and deadly.

Fingertip hovering, she cleared her throat to dislodge the sudden lump of fear. "Why not?"

"Because if you do, I'm going to tell everyone you orgasmed with me." He flattened the palm of his hand over her mound and rubbed gently. "That you lost control and took your pleasure with me repeatedly."

"You wouldn't." Her words came out in a breathless whisper, and she didn't resist him when he pressed his thighs against the outsides of her legs, trapping her. "Yes, I would." Serious dark eyes gazed at her. "I will do whatever I have to in order to convince you you're mine. That we belong together."

His words ran through her mind, and her body responded with a low throb. "Prince—"

"Call me Master." He grinned as she made a strangled noise, and nuzzled his face against her stomach. "Let me do whatever I want to you when we're alone, and I'll keep your secret."

She twisted her hands together, and her lower lip trembled as she fought back tears. Gods, she wanted what he offered so badly. She was trapped, caught as surely by her own desires as her body was held by his hands.

"We will pretend I am your Master and you are my beloved concubine." The intensity of the emotion in his stare was too much for her. She lowered her gaze and stared at his big, scarred fingers pressing into her hips. "Say yes."

Just this once, just for a few hours, she could have what she wanted. What choice did she have? He had complete control of the situation. Complete control of her. That thought made her pussy clench, and wet heat trickled down her inner thigh. Taking in a deep breath, she whispered, "Yes."

His grip on her hips tightened until she made a little sound of need. "Yes, what?"

She looked at him from beneath her lowered lashes and said the words she had wanted to say her whole life. "Yes, Master."

A tear trailed down her cheek and another followed. This was too intense, too much. Every fantasy she had ever had revolved around those words, and now she was saying them to a man who was destined to break her heart. The irony of the situation was bitter enough to choke on.

He pulled her down onto his lap and rested her face against his chest. His scent and a hint of the herbal soap he used filled her. Strong arms wrapped around her and held her close, cradling her as she cried. Confusion, desire, and the feeling of being cherished tore at her heart. Great sobs racked her body, and he held her, stroking her back and arms as her sobs tapered off to sniffles.

"I know this is hard for you." He tilted her head and gave her a kiss on her temple. "I'm proud of you for being so brave, my Concubine."

His words seared a path through her sorrow, soothed her pain, and made her heart ache with an emotion she dared not name. With slow movements, he kissed his way down her cheek until his lips brushed against hers in a soft kiss that tasted like her tears. Her breath came out in a soft gasp, and her body started to warm beneath his hands.

He must have felt the change, because his strokes along her back and arms slowed and grew teasing. "Can anyone get in here without your permission?"

Unable to speak, her throat raw from crying, she shook her head. He nodded and easily lifted her in his arms as he rose from the chair, carrying her to the bathroom. She stole a glance at herself in the mirror and winced. Her eyes were almost swollen shut from crying, and her nose was red and raw.

He sat her on the edge of the giant tub and turned on the faucets.

"What are you doing?"

"I'm taking care of my property."

"Oh," she said in a soft whisper. It was the only answer she could come up with. As he fiddled with the temperature, getting the water right, she found herself becoming more and more aroused. The way he was taking such care with preparing the water for her made that emotion she wouldn't name surge inside her. She parted her thighs slightly as her body responded to his nearness.

The tub quickly filled, and he pulled her up by her hands. He stripped off her robe with an efficient tug of her belt. She trembled as his hands skimmed down over her shoulders and traced the outer curves of her breasts. Her nipples pebbled into stiff peaks, and her heart thudded as his hands continued to circle her breasts.

"Into the bath with you," he said in a rough voice and picked her up as if she weighed no more than a feather. The warm water embraced her and did nothing to dispel the arousal his touch had built within her. Her breath came out in a soft moan of need as he pulled off his shirt. Muscles, big and firm, covered with scars and tan skin. The soft, dark hair on his chest narrowed and led down to the impressive bulge of his erection behind his black pants.

A deep sense of satisfaction filled her as she sank into the water up to her neck. After a lifetime of never being good enough, beautiful enough, it delighted her to be with a man who obviously found her desirable. Even in her current tear-streaked state.

Reminded of her appearance, she quickly grabbed a washcloth and squeaked as his hand closed over hers. "Lay back."

Her body complied even before her mind processed his words, and his dark gaze warmed with satisfaction. He wet the washcloth with a bar of rose-colored soap and worked up a good handful of suds. He took her arm firmly in his calloused hand and rubbed the cloth over her neck and shoulders.

The soft scrape of the cloth over her sensitized skin had her wriggling, and he chuckled. "Stand."

She hesitated, then scrambled to her feet when his soapy fingers closed over the bump of her nipple and squeezed hard. The shocking pain blended with her desire, and her clit grew hard and erect. Wet and dripping, she stared down at him as he ran the washcloth over her thighs and hips.

"Spread your legs."

She moved her legs slightly apart. It was so different being on the other end of the commands, seeking to carry out the orders rather than give them. Her small burst of defiance quickly came to an end when he yanked her out of the water and over his knee.

With her wet bottom in the air, she tried to pull away. "What are you—"

His big hand smacked her bottom, and she jerked with a scream. "You will obey me." Another slap and heat radiated from her core. "You will do what I say." Two more slaps, each on different cheeks. She cursed and pushed at him, unable to escape his strength. "You have no choice. You are mine to play with, mine to care for, and mine to please." Thick fingers ran between the swollen lips of her labia, and he made a soft sound of pleasure at discovering how slick with desire she was. "Do you understand me?"

Humiliated and aroused, she wiggled slightly against his erection pressing into her stomach. "Yes, damn you."

Another slap, this time on the sensitive skin where her thigh met her bottom. "I love the way your ass turns red beneath my hand and the way your cunt heats for me." Fingernails traced over her burning skin, and she bit back a moan. "Now, what do you say?"

"Yes, Master." Gods, he was training her as surely as she had ever trained a novice. Senses long buried began to awaken, and the ever present urge to please filled her. Relaxation softened her stiff muscles, and she turned her head to place a kiss on his thigh.

"Good girl," he whispered. "Now spread your legs."

Still bent over his lap, she did as he ordered and placed her hands on the floor to brace herself. Water puddled beneath her, but her body was so aroused she didn't even feel chilled. One hand held her in place while he traced up and down the slick lips of her pussy. One side, then the other, never quite reaching her swollen nub. She tried to keep still, but her hands clenched and unclenched on the smooth marble.

Abruptly a big finger pushed inside her and stroked the sensitive walls of her pussy as his thumb ran a circle around her clit. He finger fucked her with horribly gentle thrusts while she twitched her hips in an effort to get him to touch her where she wanted, where she needed. The calloused tip of his thumb moved closer, tugging on the edge of her hood.

"Please," she moaned as tension built to the level of pain.

"Please what?" His erection jumped against her as her vagina clenched his finger.

"Please, Master, may I come?" Embarrassment heated her cheeks, but she bucked her hips on his hand as he increased his speed.

"Not yet." A second finger joined the first, stretching her while all the blood in her body seemed to rush either to her head or her clit. Her world narrowed down to him, focused on his movements until everything else faded. The breath rushed from her lungs as he stroked with increasing pressure. Her eyes closed, and she gave a little moan as he pressed on her G-spot.

"So responsive." The hand holding her in place moved, reaching down to cup her breast. "And these nipples, sweet enough to eat." He removed his fingers, and she let out a cry of protest. Aching and unfulfilled, she tried to think of the right words, the right actions to make him continue.

"Master—"

"Hush." He pinched the lips of her pussy together so that her clit stood out in a pulsing bud of need.

She hovered on the brink of orgasm. The pain from her bottom, his fingers teasing her nipple, and the slow slide of his palm against her pussy all combined into a deep pleasure that left her shuddering.

He gave her mound a tiny slap and shifted and held his hand pressed to her clit. "You may use my hand to come."

With a strangled groan, she rocked her hips as best she could on his lap, pushing herself up on her arms and straining. A hard grind against his hand and the first bright spark of her orgasm had her screaming. She pressed herself against his hand and grew dizzy as her body jerked in time with the deep contractions of her orgasm. Two fingers thrust into her, stroking her gently and enjoying the rippling grip of her vagina. So good, she let herself be held by him as she came with shivers and moans. When the last ounce of pleasure was wrung from her body, he swung her around onto his lap and cradled her in his arms.

Floating, she shifted as her bottom burned against his legs. The world tilted as he stood, grabbing a towel and wrapping her up in it. Sleepy, warm, and utterly spent, she ran her fingers over his chest and idly stroked the soft hair there. His heartbeat was slow and sure against her ear as hers still raced. Using his elbow, he dimmed the lights until the room was bathed in a soft warm glow.

He gently lowered her back onto the sapphire blue cover of her bed. With firm hands, he unwrapped the towel from her body and examined her. The hunger in his eyes stirred her desire like a lazy hand, and she stretched out before him, displaying herself for his eyes. He was her Master, and she lived to serve.

"Such a beautiful little body. So perfectly shaped for my pleasure." He thought she was beautiful. She turned her head to the side and willed herself not to cry. What was it about this man that brought her emotions so close to the surface? Whenever she was around him, everything seemed enhanced, richer somehow.

He stroked himself through his pants, and she parted her thighs for him in invitation, eager for the rush of his orgasm. Already his hormones flavored the air with a delicious spice. She pouted as he shook his head. "Not yet."

He looked around the room and frowned. "Let's see..." Rubbing a finger against his wrist cuff, he gave her a glance that curled her toes. "Release my wrist cuffs."

Shocked, she tried to sit up, only to have the breath leave her lungs in a rush as he pounced on her. He pressed his groin to hers and pinned her as she tried to wiggle away from him. "Concubine, remove my cuffs."

"I can't do that," she said in a scandalized whisper.

"Yes, you can. And you will. Or are you breaking our bargain?" He watched her carefully, a small, triumphant smile crinkling the fine lines around his eyes as she tried to push him off.

He captured her wrists in his big hands and held them above her and nuzzled his face against her cheek.

The rough scrape of his stubble sizzled along her skin, and the pressure of his body on hers awoke the stinging throb of her spanked bottom. Instead of cooling her desire, his actions only put her into a deeper state of need.

"If I do, a signal will be sent, and Pimina will call me, demanding to know what is going on." Pressure began to build in her core again, and she wiggled beneath him.

"Well, that would put a damper on things." He moved his pelvis in time with the rocks of her hips until she began to pant. "Keep your hands above your head." His lips brushed against her ear, and he continued to kiss their way down her neck, stopping at the curve of her collarbone. Teeth nipped her, and she moaned for him. "You like a little pain, don't you?"

Blushing, she nodded and fisted her hands together above her head.

"I didn't hear you." Slow and wet, his tongue traced down her chest to the swell of her small breast. She tensed and waited for the disappointment she'd had from all her partners at the size of her chest. *"Pitiful." "Midget." "You look like a boy."* The words of displeasure from everyone around her when her body failed to develop into the prized plump and tall beauty of her people. Even worse, the memory of the wilting erection of her first lover when she'd stood naked before him. She closed her eyes so she wouldn't have to see the discontent in his gaze. "Yes, Sir."

"You know, I've always loved your breasts." He cupped one in his big hand, rolling the taut nipple beneath his thumb. "Round, perfectly shaped, and utterly delicious. And oh so soft." He captured her nipple and swirled his tongue around the peak. A hard suck had her lifting beneath him, and his chuckle rumbled through her skin to her heart. "Did I mention how much I enjoyed how responsive you are?"

Her reply fled her mind as he started to toy with her other nipple. Her life narrowed down to the hard, painful tugs of his fingers followed by the soothing lick of his tongue. Pain followed by pleasure; punishment followed by reward. Arms shaking, she wrapped her legs around him and ground her pussy against the hard erection trapped behind his pants.

Rolling over to the side, he pulled her to him and took her mouth in a kiss that left no doubt of his need. With his lips still pressed against hers, he started to play with her outer labia, soft strokes that quickly drove her out of her mind. Her body ached, hurt for his cock. She strained to pull him closer and wrapped her arms around his neck. She ran her hands over the delicious silk of his skin and enjoyed the sensation of burying her hands in his hair.

With a deep growl, he flipped her over onto her belly and gave her sore bottom a swat that made her yell. "I said hands over your head."

"I'm sorry, Master." She quickly placed her cheek down onto the bedcover and stretched her arms out in front of her. Big hands lifted her bottom, and cool air moved over her exposed pussy.

"Goddess, your cunt is redder than your ass." A knuckle ran through her wet folds, and she shuddered.

"I'm going to fuck you now, Concubine. If you move your arms one inch, I will stop."

She lifted her hips higher in a silent invitation. The bed rolled as his weight shifted, and she wanted to look and see what he was doing but was afraid he would stop. Straining to hear, to feel him, she yelled as he grabbed her hips and jammed as much of his cock into her as he could. It took all her willpower to keep her hands in front of her as her swollen pussy stretched to take him. She let out a small whimper of pain as he pulled her hips and filled her until his balls slapped against her clit.

"So tight." His cock jerked within her, and her body clenched around him. "Your little cunt wants to suck the cum from me."

She reveled in the feeling of him moving within her. Satisfaction like she had never known broke through the last barrier around her heart, and she felt complete.

Moving slowly, he ran his hands down her back in long sweeps. "The softest skin I've ever touched." One of those hands slipped beneath her and toyed with the curls guarding her mound. "If I had the pick of all the women in the universe, I would always choose you."

Still slow and easy, he leaned forward and bit the sensitive muscle where her shoulder and neck connected. Sparks of pleasure flew through her body until she was panting and straining beneath him. He seemed to know what she needed before she was even aware of it, adjusting his pace until he was pounding into her. Fast and hard, his hand stroked over her clit, tugging at the soft hood until she keened.

"That's it," he groaned and ground his hips into her, going as deep as he could. "Come for me." Arching her back, she took as much of him as she could, trembling as her orgasm turned the world white with pleasure. A moment later he joined her, and her breath caught as the force of his orgasm burned through her. Gods, she could feel it! She could feel the dual sensations of his cock jerking inside her and the slick heat of pussy gripping him.

Unable to do more than exist, she slumped to the mattress, only held in place by the iron-hard grip of his arm. "Mine," he growled out and bit her shoulder hard enough to draw blood. "Mine."

Every muscle in her body turned to liquid, leaving her floating in a space that had no time or thought. Her awareness focused down to the beating of their hearts, the rush of blood trickling from her shoulder into his mouth. As he withdrew from her, she managed to make a little sound of protest. Never had she experienced such passion, followed by a contentment that wrapped her heart and soul in dizzying warmth. She sank into that feeling of bliss and let herself fully relax in his arms. Her mind felt fuzzy, as if she had drunk too much wine, and it was hard for her to form a coherent thought, so she just gave up and let herself enjoy.

Moments later, his wrist pressed to her mouth, and she tasted blood. Opening her dazed eyes, she found he had bit his wrist and pressed the wound to her lips. "Taste me," he commanded, and her mouth opened of its own accord. A delicate lick revealed a complex taste of copper and sweetness she had never experienced before. Rich, alive, his essence flowed into her and filled the void in her heart completely.

After pulling his wrist away from her eager tongue, he tucked them both beneath the blankets and held her close. No words were spoken, just soft and slow explorations of each other's bodies. She had no idea how much time had passed before her mind began to surface from its blissed-out daze. His skill in bed had astounded her, and considering she had spent the last hundred years learning the art of pleasure, that was saying something.

The unwelcome thought of him sharing himself like this with another woman tried to intrude, and she was surprised by her own savage reaction. Her heart lurched with adrenaline, and her fingers curled into claws. She would kill anyone who tried to take him from her. He was hers. A small part of her mind, growing louder by the second, vehemently protested that notion with a soul-chilling fear. She wanted to ignore it, to bury it beneath an ocean of his love.

Her fists gripped his hair, pulling his mouth toward hers as she gave him a kiss that stirred his cock against her belly. His hungry rumble of satisfaction soothed her as he broke the kiss and breathed gently into her face. The scent of his breath calmed her instantly, and she went soft in his arms.

She closed her eyes so tightly she saw stars and pushed a hand at his chest. This wasn't right; she shouldn't be feeling this way. "Prince—"

"Shhhh," he whispered and blew another warm breath across her lips. Once again her body relaxed against him even as her mind raced.

"What did you do to me?" She tried to move away, but he pulled her close, and her heart surged with joy at his touch.

In a tone reeking with satisfaction, he said, "I bonded you."

"You what?"

Chapter Nine

His hands clamped on her wrists and pinned her to the bed when she tried to move away. Her mind raced as she struggled to put a meaning to his words. Bonded? What the hell was that? Pimina had never mentioned anything called bonding. She stared at him in shock while he gave her a smile filled with such tenderness that it melted her heart even as her mind tried to absorb the changes to her body. She felt...complete. It would have been an amazing sensation if she didn't also feel like she was going crazy. He was inside her, filling her mind and body, his presence growing stronger with every beat of her heart.

"When men of my race find our mate, we release chemicals in our blood that physically bond her to us. Our minds, our souls are joined as one. Even now the chemistry of your brain is changing to better sync with mine, and my body is changing to respond to your desires. You are my woman now, and I'll never have another. I'm not physically capable of breeding with another woman without your consent." He nuzzled her cheek, and she fought the urge to melt into his embrace.

His words echoed in her mind as she tried to come to terms with what he'd just told her. He'd manipulated her, torn down the carefully erected walls around her heart, and made it impossible for her to deny her feelings. That bastard. "Are you insane? How dare you bond me against my will!" Deep hurt shone in his eyes before he turned away from her. She immediately wanted to take back her words and soothe his pain, but her panic and anger wouldn't let her.

"How dare you hold me against my will." He sat up on the bed and glowered down at her. "At least I bonded you because I lo—care about you. The only reason you're with me is because it's your job."

His words stung, and she scrambled out of bed, pulling her ratty, discarded robe on. "Do you know what you've done? You've signed our death warrant! How am I supposed to help you attract the attention of the empress when the thought of you even looking at another woman makes me insane with jealousy?" She didn't add that she had felt this way even before they bonded. Right now she wanted to hurt and scare him into seeing reason. If he kept up with this insane notion of their being together, they would both die.

Her legs shook too much to hold her weight, and she sank to the floor. He made a distressed noise and slid off the bed, kneeling next to her and stroking her back. Damn him, but his touch soothed her like a thousand hot baths. Even her terror receded beneath his touch until she was able to find a small island of calm amid the ocean of her fear.

"It doesn't have to mean our deaths." His lips brushed against her cheek, and she turned away from him. It was the only thing she could do. Her body didn't want to leave his touch. "Help me escape. Come with me."

"I can't!" Her breath choked in her throat, and she weakly slapped away his hand as he brushed a tear away. Oh how he tempted her. For a brief moment, she actually considered it, but quickly realized they would never make it. Layers and layers of security measures kept Kyrimia safe from invaders and kept her people prisoner. The muscles in her body stiffened as she considered that new thought. It had never occurred to her to want to leave. Raised on tales from the regulators about the horrors of the rest of the galaxy, she had been grateful for the defenses that kept them safe. Now, thanks to Devnar, that illusion had been ripped away as well.

"You can, and you will." His voice grew hard, and he cupped her chin in his hand, forcing her to meet his dark gaze. "You will help me escape, and you will come with me."

"No." Her voice came out in an agonized whisper that made him flinch. They couldn't escape; it was impossible. They would both die or spend the rest of their lives in constant torture working in the zanthin mines. The only way he was going to survive is if she loved him enough to let him go.

"Melania, I can't live without you." His thumbs brushed away her tears, and she leaned into his touch. Hating him and wanting him in a mixture of emotions that made her feel like she was losing her mind. "Even if I wanted to, I can't—and not because of the bond. I want you for my woman. I want you to have my children and be my mate."

A bitter laugh worked out of her throat, and he pulled back. "I've been sterilized. I can't have children without the empress's permission."

"I know," he said and pulled her back onto the bed with him. "We'll find a way to fix it."

"Idiot, only the empress has the chemicals that are needed to undo the change," she spat out and held her heart. Its ache doubled, and she felt an echo of his hurt. She clutched her head and moaned. "Get out of my mind."

"I'm sorry." Sorrow layered his words, but the grief coming off him eased. "You will have to learn how to manage our bond. Once you're trained in how to block me, it will get better. I'll do my best to not overwhelm you with my feelings."

"I hate you," she said in a dull voice. "You've destroyed my life." It killed her heart to say that, but she had to stop this before it went too far. A bitter laugh escaped her as she clutched her head and realized they had already gone way beyond the point of no return.

Silence stretched between them, and he gathered his clothes. The rustle of fabric over skin sounded loud to her ears, and she wallowed in her misery. His sadness receded, replaced with a sense of purpose and strength.

"Melania, you have to pull yourself together."

"Why?" she said in a dull voice. "We're dead."

Muttering an oath, he took her shoulders in his hands, forcing her to look at him. "We are not dead. We are only dead if you give up on me."

Oh how his words stung. She had never given up on anyone, ever. As a breaker, she had been given the most damaged hearts and bodies and, through sheer willpower, had managed to heal them. It was time to remember who she was and what she had to do. She held his gaze while pressing on her bracelet and said, "The maid will take you back to your room."

He sighed and stroked her face. "If we were on my planet, we would be celebrating our bonding with a party you could not imagine. My family would all be there, eager to welcome you into our home and our lives." Homesickness, love, and contentment radiated from him, and she could only stare as he continued. "They would love you, my sister and mother especially. Think about it, Melania. Think about all the things you could have if you were only brave enough to try."

A chime sounded at the door, and he stepped back. "Secure my wrists."

She averted her eyes and listened to the metallic *snick* as his cuffs snapped together. She stood and said, "Attend." The sight of him falling to his knees before her felt wrong. She should be the one kneeling.

Rebellious thoughts filled her head, and she struggled for control as she strode over to the door and opened it. Salina stood on the other side, and her lips thinned into an angry line as she took in Melania's tearstained face. "Mistress, how may I be of service?"

Guilt radiated from Devnar, and she glanced over her shoulder. It was odd to be able to read his every emotion without having to search for the clues in his face. "Take him back to his rooms and see that he is fed. Tomorrow we are going to the Golden Arena."

"Thank you, Mistress," he said in a soft voice and stood. With his eyes lowered like a proper novice, he stood next to Salina and waited patiently.

"Good night, Novice." His longing for a kiss moved through her, and she actually took a step toward him before her mind kicked in. Gritting her teeth, she gave Salina a smile that did nothing to soothe the other woman's worry. She slammed the control panel next to the door and shut it in their faces. Sorrow and fear churned in her stomach as she leaned back against the wall and slumped to the floor.

What was she going to do?

* * *

After weeks of isolation, the roar of the crowd sped Devnar's pulse and deepened his embarrassment. Naked except for a jeweled silver collar and his ever-present wrist cuffs, he followed Melania on a glittering leash, the black marble floors shot with streaks of bronze cold beneath his bare feet. He kept his gaze locked on her lithe back and tried to ignore the speculative looks and whispers that followed in their wake.

Melania's tension rolled through him, mixing with his own until he didn't know where his nervousness ended and hers began. He had to get control of himself for her sake. If they kept feeding each other's fear, it could quickly snowball out of control and render them both useless. He took a controlled breath and eased his muscles. Pulling back from his bond was one of the hardest things he'd ever done, but he closed off his side of the connection as much as he could. Big emotions would still leak through, but it should give her some sense of privacy.

Pausing, Melania tugged at the leash, and he stopped next to her. All his efforts to speak with her had been met with silence. When he continued to try to reason with her, she had threatened to gag him. That didn't stop the complex rush of feelings coming from her. With her refusal to speak, she had given him time to assess and get comfortable with their bond. Fear and determination were her primary emotions, but beneath was the ever-present glow of her love for him. Though he was sure she would deny it with everything she had, he knew she loved him.

The bonded men he knew always bragged about what it was like to make love to a bond mate, saying it was the ultimate pleasure. Devnar had doubted them at the time, but now he knew it was true. Just the idea of feeling her emotions as she orgasmed around his cock had him hard and throbbing. He would know exactly what she wanted and how to pull the most pleasure from her body and mind. Last night she had been a wild little thing in bed, undone by his commands and restraints. Dominating her had excited him as much as it had excited her, and he couldn't wait to see what else he could get his reluctant little concubine to do. As he had thought about their time together last night, her lips had softened, and he caught her peeking at him out of the corner of her eye.

Despite her apparent indifference, he could still smell her desire for him. Even if she was determined to punish herself, her body didn't want him to go. Unconsciously, she turned her small frame toward his. His body wanted nothing more than to take her into a dark alley and plunge into her silken heat. Fortunately his mind recognized the danger that would put his mate in and allowed him to control his base urges.

The fact that she radiated fear like she was in danger made him even more edgy, and he had to strain to control his temper. Every man who stepped near her was viewed as a potential challenge. He leaned closer and took in a deep breath of her scent, seeking to calm himself with the knowledge that she smelled clean and healthy. The wash of her hormones did the trick, and his instincts mellowed out enough to allow him to work on keeping his emotions shielded from her.

Damn, it was a lot harder to separate himself from her than he'd thought it would be.

She looked up at him, and love surged through their bond. He knew he was grinning like a fool, but he couldn't help it. Her love was his joy. The great dome echoed with thousands of conversations, and he had to duck to hear her low voice. "You're doing very well, Prince."

Her praise warmed him, and he stepped closer, pressing his body next to hers. She started to move away, then sighed and relaxed into him. That little bit of surrender to his will made his cock jerk. "Thank you, Mistress."

She glanced down at his erection, and a slight smile curved her lush lips. With her nutmeg brown hair pulled back into an elaborate braid, the strong beauty of her face left him breathless. If being the perfect slave was going to keep her at his side, he would do that. She would have no reason to complain, and it would give him time to escape with her.

"What can I do to please you, Mistress?"

Her eyebrows rose, and he noticed for the first time that she used some kind of cosmetic to darken her eyelashes. She glanced down at his cock again, and her lust washed over him. "You may not be so eager to please once you see what is in store for you."

He waited until her gaze returned to his face. Their eyes met, and he tried to put his whole heart into his words. "As long as you're by my side, I can survive anything."

Pleasure and guilt flowed through their bond, along with a hint of determination. She looked away and tugged on his leash. "Come."

Obediently he followed behind her as they wove through the crowd. There were a few other slaves in the mass of people, but most of the patrons were fully dressed and obviously wealthy. Jewels sparkled in the dim sunlight, and everywhere he looked, there were inhumanly beautiful people. Surrounded by all their physical perfection, he couldn't help but feel a small worm of self-doubt twist in his stomach. Could Melania ever really be happy on his planet? Jensia was technologically advanced, but his people preferred wild nature to groomed perfection. Would she be accepting of living in a palace among the trees or fearful of all that open space?

Merchants lined the entrance to the arena, and he was interested to see that while they were all beautiful, they weren't quite as perfect. Here a nose a little too big for a man's face, there a woman with a gap in the front of her teeth. The young, plump merchant selling some type of delicious-smelling bowls of soup had deep acne scars.

A richly dressed man with short blond hair and a dark-skinned woman moved through the crowd. In front of them, a pair of guards in dark jade green leathers cleared a path for them. A small hush of conversation followed in their wake, and he lifted his head to see what the commotion was.

Between them, a beautiful little girl with her mother's dark hair and her father's gray eyes giggled and held her parents' hands. Pride and joy radiated from the pair, and everyone who saw them smiled. It was obvious the little girl was adored, but he didn't miss the look of envy on many of the faces in the crowd.

Melania hid her face from him and quickly led him through the crowd. An intense longing and sadness flowed from her, and he wanted to take her in his arms and let her know he would take care of her. When he reached for her, she hissed, "Stop. Remember who you are while we are in public, Novice." Her words stung, and she glanced back over her shoulder with a small smile. "I'm doing my best not to drag you off into some dark corner and let you have your wicked way with me. Try to be a little less appealing." She licked her lips and lowered her voice further. "Those men and women in the sparkling white leathers? They are regulators. You must not do anything to draw their attention." She adjusted his collar with trembling hands. "I can do nothing to protect you from them if you so much as give them a dirty look. Please behave for both our sakes."

Though his pride rebelled at the thought of being submissive to anyone, his need to protect his mate overrode his natural arrogance. "I'll be your perfect concubine."

Her lips twitched as she fought a smile. "Just keep your eyes on the ground and your mouth shut, please."

He bowed. "I live to serve."

She rolled her eyes, and he was glad to note that some of the tension left her shoulders as she led them into the long line winding into the arena. From a series of elevated tables, a line of men and women in glittering white leathers controlled the crowd entering the arena. Without being obvious, Devnar studied them as Melania fell into line behind an older pair of women gossiping with each other. After he realized they weren't talking of anything useful, he tuned them out and focused on the rest of the crowd. Mostly unarmed, with a few personal guards in their jade green leathers here and there.

What interested him was how everyone grew tense as they approached the regulators. He tried to see what was so intimidating, but they looked like the normal Kyrimian perfection to him. All tall, plump women and muscular men of different ages and coloring. The weapons at their sides raised his eyebrows, but not as much as the metal whips draped over the backs of their chairs. With razor tips, the whips would rend the flesh off the bone if used with force.

"Do they really whip people?" he asked in a low breath as their line inched forward.

Melania barely nodded and pulled him down to fiddle with his collar, tugging out strands of hair that had got trapped beneath it. "Depends on the severity of the crime. For small infractions like straying by accident into a royal section of town, I would get a few strokes with just the whip." Her fingers pressed to the back of his neck. "For something like trying to impersonate royalty, I'd pick a limb and they would whip it with the razors until that limb fell off. Then I'd be reduced to worker rank."

The line shuffled forward, and she stepped away from him with a serious expression darkening her beautiful face. "Don't speak unless spoken to. Don't stare at them, and for the love of the Gods, please don't do anything to attract attention to yourself."

The chatter of the elderly women ahead of them silenced, and Devnar watched the purple sheen of Melania's black boots as she shuffled forward. He had never paid so much attention to feet before and found that her small feet stood out among her taller and heavier-boned people. He thanked the Goddess that her delicate frame was what had saved her for him.

"Greetings, Breaker," a woman said in an ice-cold voice.

"Greetings, Regulator." Melania tugged at his leash, and he took a small step forward. "I've brought this novice to be displayed at Lady Grenba's command."

Murmured words in a language he couldn't understand came from the regulator. That puzzled him. The translator implanted in his ear should be able to translate any of the nine thousand known languages of this galaxy. The regulator must be using a secret language known only to other regulators. That knowledge combined with the other bits and pieces he had learned of them led him to believe the regulators held a lot more power on this planet than he'd first thought. Maybe as much as their royalty.

Musing this, he missed the fact that they were being let through, and stumbled after Melania. The regulator made a small sound of disgust, and Melania's shoulders grew tight, but she hurried them through the crowd in an almost run. She only slowed after they were well across the square and deep into the crowd.

They stopped before an elaborate black stone fountain. Melania sat down on the edge and pretended to check the fastening of her boot. "That was close. The regulator was suspicious about you, but Lady Grenba must have smoothed your entrance."

"What do you mean?" he murmured and fought the urge to scan the crowd at his back. No need to draw any more attention to him than being a naked man on a leash already did. Still, knowing a potential enemy was near made the skin between his shoulder blades crawl. He found himself staring at a handsome older man with silver hair who watched them. A quick glance down at Melania showed she was still fiddling with her boot, and when he looked back, the man was gone.

"You have no file, no history. If the regulator had run you, it would have been apparent that you're an off-worlder. While you're here on official decree, they could have...questioned"—a wave of fear rushed through their bond and made the hair on his arms stand up—"us about who you are and why you're here. People have been known to not survive the gentle persuasions of the regulators. Royalty and servant alike."

"I see," he said. He burned to ask her more, but this was not the place for it. No, the longer they were here, the more he wished to be back at the relative safety of her home. It grated on his nerves and pride that he had to allow his mate to be in such danger, and that he was part of the problem. "So the bitch pulled some strings and got us in."

"Yes." Melania stood and stroked his arm in a featherlight touch. He felt her relax as she took a deep breath. "Now let's go display you before the bitch gets impatient and comes looking for us."

He clenched his hands into fists in an effort to keep from reaching out and touching her. If they had been on Jensia, they would still be in his bed, glorying in the satisfaction of their bond. That knowledge did nothing to ease his temper or Melania's worry. He obviously wasn't going to escape from this place, so he had to bide his time and stay with Melania until they returned to her home, where they stood a better chance. Maybe he could get her to give him access to the maps and information they would need for a getaway. If she resisted, he'd just have to tie her up and withhold her orgasm until she relented. Ahead of him, she stumbled as his lust that accompanied his thought hit her. She turned to glare at him, but he gave her his best innocent look. It didn't work on her any better than it had worked on his mother, and he grinned as she rolled her eyes at him.

The crowd around them became denser as they walked through a set of gigantic metal arches. Inscribed on the dark metal were scenes of men and women fighting strange creatures he didn't recognize. Melania coughed, and he lowered his eyes to the ground again.

The smooth tiles beneath their feet changed to white marble, and he glanced up to get his bearings. They entered a white marble square with several raised platforms that flanked the entrance to the arena. Tall trees in gigantic metallic pots lined the square, throwing shadows on the crowd that ebbed and flowed. More guards in subdued jade green leathers constantly scanned the packed square. Their presence made his shoulders go tight.

Small alcoves with pillow-strewn benches lined the square. Many of them were occupied by groups of men and women covered in glittering jewels and shimmering silk robes. Here and there, naked men and women dallied on the ends of leashes, each very attractive in their own perfect way. At the far end of the open space, a long corridor led into a massive arena.

One space was already occupied by a plump blonde woman locked in a stockade. With her legs spread open, her wet pussy was exposed for all to see. A group of well-dressed men and women stood in front of her, laughing as she squirmed when her male trainer gave her round bottom a slap. Her answering moan of pleasure made her trainer smile with pride, and he stroked her wet slit until she bucked against his hand.

Is that what he was here for? To be put on exhibit like some animal? The thought churned his stomach, and he tried to fight his rising panic.

Devnar froze, pulling against the leash in Melania's hand. She turned to see what had made him stop, and a look of sympathy briefly crossed her face, but she said in a cold voice, "Attend."

He tried to fight his panic and sank to his knees. "Please, Mistress, I—"

Cupping his cheek, she stroked her fingers over his lips, and he licked her passing flesh. A flash of desire washed through him, and she sighed softly. "I am going to display you, Devnar. I'm going to let everyone see that magnificent body, dream about touching your thick cock." She pressed her thumb into his mouth, letting him suck on it as her voice grew husky. "They are going to talk about you, wonder who you are, and how they can acquire you." She closed her eyes and whispered, "And I'll be watching you, pretending you are mine."

He bit the tip of her thumb, and her thighs pressed together as she removed it from his mouth. "I am yours."

Anger flashed through her eyes, but the pain and longing she felt passed through their bond. "Unless you want to see me tortured, you will keep that sentiment to yourself while we are here."

"Don't leave me, and I will." He challenged her with his gaze, not letting her break eye contact with him.

A man's voice cut through the din of conversation in the square. "Breaker Melania, who is that exotic creature you're playing with?"

Melania's eyes grew huge with fear. She nodded slightly at Devnar and breathed out. "I won't leave you. But you must behave. Please."

She waited until he nodded, then tugged his leash and led him across the square. They stopped before a tall man in long bronze robes embroidered with shimmering gold thread on the shoulders. With long silver hair pulled back with a gold thong, the thin man's hands flashed and sparkled as the rings on his fingers captured the light. A small group of men and women in various colored robes surrounded him, and they all watched Devnar far too closely for his comfort. Despite their well-manicured appearances, he saw every one of them as a threat. It was something in the way they stood, in the intelligence in their eyes. These were hawks pretending to be peacocks. He studied the man in the bronze robe and changed his opinion. No, not hawks. They were like a pride of lions, and this was their leader.

His tension ratcheted up another level until his jaw hurt from clenching it. Despite their soft robes and carefully styled hair, all of these people radiated dominance and danger. But none as much as the silver-haired man that now examined him and Melania. The way he constantly scanned his surroundings reminded Devnar of his old war instructor. Always ready for an attack no matter where they were.

Melania gave a low bow and jerked at his leash. At a loss of what to do, he sank to his knees and kept his gaze focused on the ground. He must do nothing to cause them concern, nothing to put Melania in danger. A bead of sweat trailed down his cheek, and he resisted the urge to brush it away.

"Lord Mithrik," Melania said in a low and clear voice.

"Interesting novice you have." The edge of the man's bronze robes entered Devnar's field of sight, and he tensed as his chin was lifted by a pair of strong fingers. Dark hazel eyes examined him, and he gripped his hands into fists as he almost lost the battle to stand and put himself between Melania and this lord. Whoever this man was, he was very dangerous.

"Fascinating bone structure. Don't you agree, Khilam?"

Khilam? The novice he'd shared with Melania?

Lord Mithrik stroked his chin with a small grunt. Fear and anger from Melania, but no surprise. What was going on?

Devnar flinched in the man's fingers still holding his chin as Khilam separated himself from the group of people and strode up with an arrogant roll of his hips. Lord Mithrik drew back, and Khilam filled his vision. Gone was the submissive novice from the day before, and in his place stood a haughty and powerful man. Dressed in tight dark emerald green pants and a soft cream shirt, his brown skin gleamed in the sunlight. Golden hoops hung from his ears, and an emerald ring as big as his pinky nail sparkled in the lights. Devnar felt even more exposed as the man he had shared a bed with stood over him and brushed a strand of his hair off his face with a gentle touch.

Khilam's familiar desire rolled over him, and his cock throbbed in response. A sudden flash of heat from Melania, and her pulse of need let him know the sight of them together aroused her. Helpless against his primitive nature, Devnar leaned into the other man's touch and rubbed his cheek into his scent. Whatever his mate wanted, he wanted. And to be honest, even without Melania's desire, he would have been attracted to the handsome man.

"Why, I think he likes you." Lord Mithrik chuckled, and the surrounding group joined in his laughter. Heat burned in his cheeks as he realized the crowd around him had grown. Using the tip of his boot, Lord Mithrik spread his legs farther apart so his balls hung low and full under his stiff erection.

"Breaker, my Steward fancies your novice. How much for him?"

Devnar stared at Melania as she tried to compose herself. Her panic burned through him, and he tried to shut her out the best he could. "Your lordship, he is not ready for service yet."

"Nonsense." Khilam continued to stroke his face, and Lord Mithrik's eyes danced with amusement at Devnar's obvious discomfort. "He responds beautifully. Not everyone likes the life beaten out of their concubines. What pleasure house does he belong too?"

Toying with his chain, Melania said in a low voice, "He belongs to Lady Grenba."

The hum of the crowd filled the silence that stretched over their small group. He lifted his chin just enough so that he could see their faces through the fringe of his lashes.

"Pity," Lord Mithrik said in a dry voice. "I'd hate to see this one broken under her hand." He watched Melania carefully, and only the slightest tightening around his eyes betrayed his impatience as she kept her silence. "In fact, Lady Grenba's watching us from across the square with a few regulators." He raised his hand in a wave, and Devnar tried to see through the crowd but could only observe the closed-off wall of pants and skirts surrounding them. "Perhaps I should... Hmm, she just entered the arena. Maybe she didn't see us."

Lord Mithrik hooked his fingers into Devnar's collar and raised him to his feet. He tensed beneath the man's hands, then let out a sigh of relief when Lord Mithrik stepped back. That relief was short-lived as Khilam spoke up, "May I sample him? You did bring him here to be displayed, didn't you?"

Melania gave a stiff nod. "Of course, Steward."

Devnar stiffened as Khilam pressed into him, and he felt the swell of the other man's cock rubbing against his. Slowly, deliberately Khilam brushed his full lips over Devnar's. A woman laughed softly as Devnar clamped his lips together, denying Khilam's tongue access. Melania's desire pushed against him. He gritted his teeth in an effort to keep from pulling her between them like she wanted.

Khilam ran his hands down Devnar's back, keeping him fully pressed against his body. "What a disappointment."

Devnar's head jerked as Melania pulled on his chain with a sharp tug. "Novice, pleasure him."

Shame and desire mixed in his blood, rushing to his aching cock as Khilam shifted his hips. The soft cloth of Khilam's pants rubbed against him, reminding him of the silk of the other man's grip. He didn't know what kind of game they were playing, but he would be damned if he was going to let Khilam make Melania angry at him.

Aware of her gaze on him, Devnar traced his hand over Khilam's jaw and cupped the back of his head. Khilam's eyes grew wide with alarm and then closed in a soft sigh as Devnar captured his lips. The bonds holding his wrists together came undone, and he took the silent hint, reaching around to grip Khilam's firm ass and pull him closer until their erections ground against each other.

Hot and hard, Khilam made soft, needy noises as Devnar stroked his tongue across Khilam's lips. Goddess, he tasted good. Masculine and warm with a hint of spice. The memory of sharing his seed with Melania brought a rush of blood to Devnar's erection that left him light-headed. Deepening their kiss, he shifted enough to allow Khilam's hand to slip between them and pull gently at the hairs around his cock. The hum of the crowd faded under a rush of Melania's desire, and he reached out to pull her toward them.

When only air met his seeking hand, he pulled back from Khilam with a frown and held out his hand to his woman. Wetting her lips with the tip of her tongue, she ever so slightly shook her head in a negative gesture. The flash of a man's rings momentarily blinded him, and he stiffened as an unfamiliar hand pressed down on his shoulder, forcing him to his knees.

"And you say he isn't ready," Lord Mithrik scoffed in a loud voice. Trumpets blared over the square, and people began to flow toward the arena. Melania pulled him to his feet with a jerk of the leash and subtly put herself between him and Khilam.

"I assure you, my lord, when he is available, I will let you know."

Lord Mithrik gave Khilam a sharp glance. "Please do. It seems as if he's had quite an effect on my Steward." Khilam shuddered in a visible effort to control himself and gave Melania an enigmatic glance.

With that, Lord Mithrik and his followers left them standing in the middle of the square as people hurried around them, eager to get to their seats.

He leaned down and whispered into her ear, "What is going on?"

"Politics," she said in a faint voice. She gripped his hand and squeezed it. "While Khilam was kissing you, the empress and her entourage passed. Lord Mithrik and his people effectively blocked her from seeing you. Lady Grenba is going to be furious." Her strange blue and brown eyes stared into his; her fear lay heavy in his heart. Politics were always a deadly game, and he was far out of his element here. His soul demanded he protect his woman, but he didn't know how. So small and fragile. He ached to hold her in his arms. "Devnar, I can't protect you from them."

"Ahh, little Mistress, don't worry about me. It is you I'm concerned about."

"What?" She glanced around and led him behind one of the tall trees, taking shelter in the shade against the wall. "Prince, I assure you I will be fine."

She gasped as he wrapped his arms around her and lifted her off her feet for a kiss. Soft, sweet, she opened for him even as her small hands pushed at his arms. "Stop," she hissed and backed away when he set her down.

"Who is Lord Mithrik, and why was Khilam with him? I thought he was a novice."

Her bitter laugh hurt his heart. She picked up the end of his leash from where it dangled between them. "Lord Mithrik is the empress's spymaster and a very dangerous man. I have no idea why he sent Khilam to us and then made sure we were aware of who he really is."

"I hate politics," he murmured and stroked his hand down her cheek. If he lived ten thousand years, he wouldn't be able to stand next to her and not want to touch her.

"At least we have that in common. I keep as far away from politics as I possibly can." She took a deep breath and tugged on his leash. "Come, we will be expected at the arena. Be on your best behavior. After that public display with Lord Mithrik and Khilam, you can bet everyone will be very curious about you. At least Lord Mithrik's interest will help protect you from the regulators. He has a long-running feud with the regulators' High Council, but they're each too powerful to take the other out. Hopefully Lady Grenba won't be angry I didn't display you as she wished. "

"If she hurts you, I will kill her." Even though he knew how ridiculous that statement seemed when he was naked and on a leash, it didn't make it any less true. He would kill to keep his bonded female safe.

"Hush." She placed her hand over his mouth. "If anyone heard you say that, you would be tortured. Favored by Lord Mithrik or not."

Shaking his head, he followed her into the crowd.

Chapter Ten

Instead of the rows of benches that he was used to in the playhouses and meeting halls at home, this arena was lined with staggered rows of individual boxes of various sizes. Each box sat from as little as two to over a dozen people. A low wall separated each box from the next and was low enough to see over if you were standing. The boxes farthest from the arena held plain wooden chairs, while the boxes with the best views had sumptuous seating with the gleam of silver and gold brocade.

The massive walled pit of the arena was filled with black sand that faintly shimmered in the sunlight breaking through the dirty clouds beyond the dome. Currently a group of scantily clad men and women performed an elaborate acrobatic routine. Their toned bodies were painted bronze, and he couldn't help but be impressed by their skill and balance.

He started to sit in the brown suede chair next to Melania when she tugged his leash and pointed to her feet. With a derisive snort, he lowered himself next to her and pressed against her thigh. The smooth leather of her uniform barely contained the heat of her body. He promised himself that sometime soon he would make her wear them while he took her repeatedly.

At the far end of the arena, a large portion of the stands was sectioned off by a shimmering wall of white. The wall flexed and moved, and he realized it was some form of energy shield. "What's that?"

"The empress," Melania said in a low voice. On either side of them, the boxes held well-dressed spectators who drank from etched glass goblets held on trays by their servants. He became conscious of many people openly staring at them as they whispered to each other. Melania's voice interrupted his attempts to read their lips and figure out what they were saying. "She's behind that shield to help protect her from assassination attempts."

A man dressed in a navy blue robe sneered at Devnar, and he lowered his eyes to the ground to keep the man from seeing his snarl. He had to behave. Had to keep from drawing any dangerous attention. Melania's last words rolled through his mind, and he frowned. In a voice barely above a whisper, he said, "Who wants the empress dead?"

She shrugged, but the anxiety rolling off her increased. The warmth of her breath tingled in his ear as she leaned down and whispered, "There are elements of our society that wish to place their own house on the throne. Other groups wish the regulators to have more power and the royal houses less. Being the empress is a dangerous privilege."

"All the more reason you shouldn't give me to her," he whispered back. He regretted the pain his words caused her, but pressed his case. "Help me, Melania."

She wrapped her hands around his leash and pulled his head up until her lips brushed his ear. "We are being watched. If you care for me, please stop trying to get me killed."

Anger washed through him and blended with his frustration. Stubborn woman. Worse yet, she was probably right. He tried to keep his head lowered but still scanned the audience. A disconcerting number of people watched them carefully. They weren't even trying to be circumspect, instead openly staring and pointing at their box. All the attention made him increasingly uncomfortable, and he wished they had never come here today.

"Why are they looking at us?"

"Lord Mithrik made a point of singling you out. They are all wondering if it would earn them political points to see you dead or their property."

He grunted in response and tried to ignore the crowd. Melania, ever aware of his needs, cupped his cheek and turned his head to look down into the area. On the black sand below, the acrobats left to scattered applause. Lime green lights flashed through the stadium, and Melania sat forward with a low hiss.

"What is it?"

"Death sport," she spat out in disgust. "A group of criminals will fight to the death, and the last man standing gets a pardon from the empress."

Doors opened in the pit of the arena, and a dozen men came out. Some wore bits of armor, while others were bare except for a loincloth. Above the arena, a giant hologram showed the participants in detail. They were armed with all manners of weapons, and Devnar found himself leaning forward, straining against his leash. His heart gave a great thud, and a high ringing filled his ears as rage burst inside his mind in an incandescent blast of white-hot heat.

His men were down there.

The sight of Ikel and Bolin lanced through him, and his blood boiled with anger and shame. He had failed them. While he was falling in love with Melania, they had been suffering. Welts covered their bodies, and they looked like they hadn't bathed in a long time. He had sworn before the Goddess that he would rescue them, and look how they had suffered. Melania's anger and fear washed through him and fed his fury until his mind switched over to full battle mode. Rational thought gave way to a surge of emotion, and his view of the world focused down to rescuing his men and eliminating any threat to his mate.

"Novice," Melania said in a panicked whisper and tugged at his chain.

"Ikel and Bolin are down there!" His voice rose into a shout, and gasps came from the boxes next to them. Down in the arena, Ikel and Bolin squared off against a group of four other men. A sword flashed, and Ikel barely managed to dodge it before another man tried to sweep his feet out from under him.

"Novice, attend!"

Panic and fury roared through their bond and combined until he saw the world through a mask of rage. "Those are my men!" he roared and jerked the leash out of Melania's hands. "I have to save them!" He started to climb the wall when a bolt of pain from his collar dropped him. Her fear clawed at his stomach, but all he could do was focus on the hologram of Bolin crushing the head of his opponent with his spiked club. Ikel lay at his feet, unmoving and covered in blood.

Memories of growing up with Ikel, comforting each other as they went through warrior training, and even sharing a woman or two, flashed through his mind. Bolin wasn't faring much better; he was still standing, but blood gushed down his body from a wound over his eyebrow. Devnar couldn't let him die on the black sands of the arena for the amusement of a bloodthirsty crowd. He focused his rage, his disgust, his despair and blasted it into Melania's mind.

Melania's face paled as he sent all his emotions pouring through the bond, trying to make her understand, trying to make her feel what he was feeling. She stood, then wavered on her feet, and he grabbed her before she fell. With a low moan, she fumbled for her bracelet before he jerked her arms away, keeping her from restraining him.

A concerned shout came from the box next to them, but he ignored it and forced Melania to look at him. "You have to do something. Please help me!" He shook her and screamed as agony radiated from his collar. Confusion rode quickly behind the wave of debilitating pain, and he wondered how she managed to shock him without touching her control bracelet. His numb hands fell from her arms as he slid in a lump to her feet, his nerve impulses firing at random and sending hard sparks of torment through his nervous system.

Screams came from around them as he tried to lift himself from the ground. The door of their box hissed open, and Lord Mithrik's voice snapped through the air like a whip. "Seize him and the breaker."

"My Lord, please—he doesn't—" Her words clamped off to muffled screams, and Devnar tried to make his arms work. A burly guard dressed in dull green leather had her gagged and handcuffed in his arms.

Lord Mithrik raised his voice as she struggled. "You are hereby charged with treason for smuggling an off-worlder onto our planet."

The crowd gasped, and shouts of "traitor" rained down over them. One of the guards stripped off her control bracelet, and another bolt of agony from his collar made him slump back to the ground. The crowd roared as something happened in the arena, but all he cared about now was his mate.

She was in danger; he had to rescue her.

Forcing his stunned muscles to cooperate, he pushed himself off the ground and made a weak lunge at the guard holding Melania. He was easily dodged and brought flat by the collar again. His body was on fire with pain. It felt as if he were being roasted alive while nails were pounded through his bones.

A boot flipped him over, and he stared into the blank face of Khilam. The man stroked a hand over his goatee and spat on Devnar's chest. "Filthy off-worlder. What would you like done with him, my lord?"

He prayed to the Goddess for the strength to save Melania. The twitching of his nerves made him flop on the ground like a fish out of water, and he tried to roll his eyes to find her. All he could do was moan, and he heard Lord Mithrik say in a cold voice, "Take her away. I want him executed, and his body burned."

Rough hands dragged him to his feet, and he struggled weakly. Khilam stepped in front of him and gripped his hair, forcing his face up. "Say good-bye to your whore." The last thing he heard before the collar knocked him out was Melania's anguished scream and the roar of the crowd.

* * *

"It's not his fault." A familiar man's voice ricocheted through Devnar's aching skull, and he moaned. Bolin needed to shut the hell up and let him nurse off this hangover in peace. Slow to respond, his eyelids felt like they weighed a thousand pounds. Bolin's blond hair came into blurry view, but his back was covered with blood and black sand.

As he struggled to remember what they had drunk in order to get to this filthy and painful state, he carefully rolled over on his back to stare at an unfamiliar ceiling. The air tasted...odd here. None of the scents of animals or growing things. Cleaned until it had almost no scent at all.

"Devnar's fault or not, he can't be associated with you. He almost ruined everything," another man replied in a shout. That voice also triggered a memory—sensual lips framed by a dark goatee. He tried to remember while staring at the dark ivory ceiling. His limbs ached, further distracting his mind.

"Well, if you had just told him what was going on, none of this would be necessary." Something rattled, and Bolin continued in a softer voice. "Surely there was a better way to test his breaker's loyalty to the empress. I told you what would happen if you tried to separate them and they were bonded." Breath puffed out of someone's lungs in a hard *oof* as Bolin continued. "It's your fault she's nearly catatonic and being held in some shithole prison. Even worse, she believes Devnar is dead. For her, that is a fate worse than death, and she has no one around her to explain what is going on. You better hope she is as smart and strong as you say, or her mind will break, and for Devnar all will be lost."

"All the more reason we had to make sure she wasn't in on Lady Grenba's plans. If what you said about bonding was true, he would have lied to keep her safe."

Lady Grenba. That name rolled through his mind like a foul fog. Dark skin, ivory dress, beautiful face with lips covered in blood.

"You also didn't need to have his woman whipped in public. He's going to be furious when he finds out."

"We had to do something. If we didn't show the regulators we were going to punish her as an example, they would have taken her."

"She's so tiny," Bolin complained as his voice moved closer. "The prince always did like his women small and fragile." His voice grew hard. "Lord Adsel knew exactly what kind of woman would arouse his interest. Lucky for us, he didn't consider she had the heart of a warrior. I thought she was going to kill that guard she broke free from."

Tiny, fragile...his woman. Devnar closed his eyes tight and chased the memory as the confusion began to clear. He had been somewhere watching his men fight.

There was a woman with him—a woman he loved. Long hair that wrapped around his body like silk, eyes as blue as the sky—no, one eye of that startling blue, while the other eye was the color of brown velvet. Melania. The gentle burn in his chest wasn't an illusion; he was bonded.

"Where is she?" His roar sounded like the croak of a sick kitten.

"My prince!" Bolin gently helped him roll his head to the side and anxiously examined him.

"Bolin." He swallowed and tried to work some saliva down his dry throat. "Where is Melania?"

"She's safe, for the moment." Khilam moved behind Bolin and jumped back when Devnar tried to lunge at him. Sadly his launch was nothing more than a lurch followed by a painful groan and ending with him rolling on his back and fighting not to puke. They must have really fried his body with that last blast from the collar.

He managed to growl out his threat without passing out. "You prick! Where is she? What have you done with her?"

"Easy," Bolin said in a gentle tone and carefully pressed Devnar back to the bench he was lying on. Voices came from outside the doorway, and Lord Mithrik entered and took in the mood of the room with one quick glance. His shoulders straightened beneath his bronze robe, and the small muscles around his mouth grew tight.

"I told you she isn't a traitor," Bolin yelled at Lord Mithrik, then swallowed audibly when those dark hazel eyes rested on him. The silence allowed Devnar to regain some of his mind, and he decided to see if there were any weapons around. If things went to shit, he was taking Lord Mithrik with him. Bare walls, smooth furniture bolted to the ground, and even the mattress he lay on was sewn into the frame. This room was a prison in the most literal sense of the word.

"Where is she?" he repeated and struggled to sit up. He would be damned if he faced his enemy lying on his back. The now unfamiliar feeling of pants tightening around his waist had him looking down. While he was out, someone had dressed him in dark trousers and an ill-fitting, deep blue shirt. A small knife was strapped to his waist, and he checked the edge. Nice and sharp. Black leather boots adorned his feet, and then he realized the most shocking thing of all: his collar was gone.

Rolling his neck, he relished the feeling of being free. He reassessed the situation and noted how Lord Mithrik studied him, and Bolin took a respectful step back from the mature politician. Those two clearly knew one another. Khilam hovered nearby, obviously wanting to stand closer to Devnar but unsure of his welcome.

Lord Mithrik opened his hands and said in a grand voice, "Prince Devnar, on behalf of the empress, I—"

He pushed himself to his feet and almost fell flat on his face. He clenched his jaw and forced his jittering knees to lock. His muscles still twitched from the electrical shock they had given him to knock him out. "Where is she?"

"She is safe," Lord Mithrik snapped, and his perfect lips curled back in a sneer. "If you're half as smart as your men seem to think, you will shut up and listen to me."

Bolin slid next to Devnar and casually helped support his weight. "Give him a chance to explain," Bolin whispered into his ear.

Devnar closed his eyes and ran his hand over the spot where the collar used to be. Strangely enough, he missed that hunk of metal. He had come to associate it with Melania and as a sign of belonging to her. Perhaps if the Goddess was good to him, he would be able to wear it for fun while they were in bed together. The reassuring glow of Melania's soul in his heart kept him from losing his mind. She was still alive and not too far away.

He turned his entire focus on the dangerous Lord Mithrik and let him see the fury in his eyes. The older man swallowed once but nodded. Lord Mithrik was the key to finding her.

Taking his silence as permission to continue, Lord Mithrik took a seat in the chair next to the bed. "Do you swear that your breaker had no intention of using you to harm the empress? That she had no involvement in the plot by Lady Grenba to enslave the will of the empress?"

"What?" Bolin grunted as Devnar stumbled into him. "She would never do that. All she ever talked about was pleasing her. Melania lives by the rules of your planet to a tee."

"Your breaker never met or spoke with Lady Grenba?" The question was said in a casual voice, but he noted how Khilam tensed. It was getting easier and easier to read the handsome man, and that bothered Devnar. In a way, it almost reminded him of how he read Melania. If he concentrated hard enough, he could almost catch the edge of the other man's emotions. He pushed that thought away and focused on Lord Mithrik.

"Of course she did. That evil bitch chewed off some man's face in front of us in order to intimidate her." He met Lord Mithrik's gaze and willed him to see he was speaking the truth. "Melania despises Lady Grenba. She has devoted her life to healing the damage that people like her do to their slaves. Never in a million years would she be part of any of that bitch's plans."

Bolin said, "See, she's innocent. I told you the prince wouldn't bond anyone who would do that."

"Do what?" Devnar asked in a quiet growl. If they didn't produce Melania soon, he was going to see just how sharp the knife they gave him was against Lord Mithrik's throat.

"One of our spies learned Lady Grenba has been selling female workers as slaves to the southern rebels of your planet. We've found that our people can breed together, and that makes our races unique to each other. There has been some speculation that a long time ago, when Kyrimia went through the Burning Times, some of our people managed to escape in primitive spacecraft. We think your people might be some of our descendants." He ignored Devnar's growl of rage and continued, "We believe Lady Grenba's been working with your Lord Adsel and exchanging men from your planet to be used as slaves here."

"Why the hell would you want our men as slaves? You have more beautiful boys here than you know what to do with." Devnar shot Khilam a sneer as he said the last part. Instead of looking insulted, Khilam actually smiled.

Lord Mithrik leaned forward on his elbows, but there was nothing relaxing about his posture. "Because your genetics are taint-free from the radiation. Your genetic codes are almost as pure as that of the royal family without having the risk of a random mutation cropping up."

Devnar rubbed his face where a headache was brewing with a vengeance. "Explain."

"After the nuclear wars and environmental disasters that shattered our world, all but for this small continent that we barely survive on, our people were almost destroyed. One out of every three births resulted in a hideous mutation that didn't survive long. We had to begin a selective breeding program, letting only those with the cleanest and strongest genes pass along their genetic codes to the next generation. That's what the regulators were originally set up for. They were the guardians of our future."

What he said made horrible sense but didn't explain why they wanted Jensian men for breeding. "Why us? I've seen your people. They're perfect."

Lord Mithrik shifted, and his face paled. "Not quite. There are thousands of…abominations born every year despite our careful and strict protocols."

"Abominations like Melania?" he spat out in an angry voice.

Shaking his head, Lord Mithrik met his gaze, and Devnar was taken aback by the pain and fear he saw there. "No, abominations like things that ate their way out of their mother's wombs and killed the birth attendant. Things with teeth and claws, human genetics merged in some time long past with those of the native animals of our planet. Even our most careful breeding cannot avoid them. They are our curse, our burden to bear."

Devnar rubbed his chest and tried to imagine the nightmare scenario Lord Mithrik described. "Why did Melania never mention them?"

"She doesn't know. Most of the population doesn't know. How would you feel, knowing that on the other side of the continent there stood a hideous prison colony of these creatures? They are remarkably resilient to the poisonous environment and actually seem to thrive beyond the domes. It is not their fault they are alive. We do the best we can to keep them in comfort."

"Spending your entire life locked behind bars. Sounds like hell to me." He ignored Lord Mithrik's glare and turned to Khilam. "You still haven't answered why you need our seed."

"Your seed is pure. Of the three births we've recorded between your people and ours, the genetics have been perfect. For the empress to have the opportunity for a concubine who will give her perfect babies, love her and only her, and be able to defend her, your men are the ideal pick. I'm sure Lady

Grenba's been smuggling your men into the different royal houses to couples desperate for a healthy child." Khilam rested his hand on Lord Mithrik's shoulder and gave a gentle squeeze. "No one should ever have to live with the horror of losing their wife and finding out their child is a monster."

Devnar looked away from the private moment and exchanged a glance with Bolin. "That all sounds wonderful and noble, but why was I kept prisoner? If you knew something was wrong, why didn't Khilam tell me when we met for the first time instead of sleeping with me? I would have helped."

"As you know," Khilam smoothly interrupted, "you're addictive to us. I volunteered to see if there was any basis to the rumors and examine your relationship with your breaker. To see if you were truly here against your will or part of Lady Grenba's schemes."

Devnar ran his hand through his hair. "Why did Lady Grenba even bother to bring me here if she has all these slaves?"

"Because she needed your royal blood." Bolin released him as Devnar's legs grew strong enough to hold him. "Royals families from all parts of the galaxy are getting ready to send their princes and princesses to try and become the next concubine."

"Lady Grenba was going to make sure you bonded Melania, then take her away from you." Lord Mithrik nodded at his growl. "They were planning on making sure you and the empress made love, and that she would become addicted to you."

"If she had Melania, I would have done anything that evil bitch asked. All Melania would have to do is tell me to have sex with the empress, and I would do it. I would do anything to please her. Without Melania's permission, I would have been as useless as a gelding, and only Lady Grenba would have the key to making me give an addicted empress what she needed." Bolin and Khilam moved away as he paced through the small room. "But Melania had nothing to do with this. Where is she?"

"Being held in the royal prison." Lord Mithrik sat back and held up his hand. "She is safe there. If we don't hold her until her sale, the regulators would have her. And we think Lady Grenba controls them or at least a powerful section of the Council."

"Melania's being sold?" He stalked toward Lord Mithrik with his fists clenched.

Khilam moved to stand between them, but Lord Mithrik didn't move from his chair. "Yes. In three days, she will be sold to the highest bidder on one of our trade moons. To vanish and never be seen again."

"If you sell her, I will kill you and everyone you love until no one with your precious genetics walks this stinking planet."

"Good thing we're selling her to you then, yes?" Lord Mithrik's hazel eyes sparkled. "We're hoping Lady Grenba will send one of her agents to the sale and try to buy Melania. Lady Grenba will have to. Melania knows the truth and is a great risk to her well-laid-out scheme."

"So you believe me that Melania's innocent?" He relaxed his shoulders and rubbed the warm spot in his heart.

"Yes. And like I said earlier, the empress apologizes for this. She really does want to establish good relations with the rest of the galaxy, and kidnapping a prince is not the way to do it." He gave Bolin an odd look, and the other man actually blushed. "Though I do believe we've found a way to smooth things over."

Khilam cleared his throat, and Lord Mithrik pressed his lips together. "I forgot to add Khilam is now the official ambassador to your planet. He's grown very...fond of you."

Now it was Devnar's turn to shuffle while Bolin coughed into his fist, and Khilam gave him a smile that would melt a glacier. "I look forward to working with the prince and his people to help rescue our women."

Devnar sat down on the edge of his bed with a deep sigh. "You said I have three days till the auction?"

"Yes. Your second in command, Volun, is waiting for you on the trade moon. He will buy Melania and bring her back to your ship. Your face is too well-known after the spectacle at the arena."

"Volun didn't know," Bolin added quickly as he watched Devnar closely. "He's deeply ashamed of his father's actions and has vowed to hunt him down and kill him. We think Lord Adsel is in a southern rebel stronghold."

Devnar slammed his fists down on the bed. "That bastard! No wonder it seems like the rebels always knew our plans. He must have been feeding them our intelligence for years."

Fury rolled through his blood. Bolin said in a low voice, "Someday, Prince, we'll find him. And when we do, he will pay."

Clearing his throat, Lord Mithrik sat forward. "While I have the utmost sympathy for your situation, we need to focus on the present. There is much to be discussed, not the least of which is organizing the rescue of our women from your planet. We're going to need your help, Prince."

He rubbed his face and looked at Bolin. "Where is Ikel?"

To his surprise, Bolin actually flushed. "He...ah...that is..." Bolin glanced at Lord Mithrik. "Ikel is being taken care of right now. He had a few injuries from the fight but he is in tender hands."

Lord Mithrik actually growled, and Khilam choked on his laughter. Devnar pressed on his throbbing temples and tried to will his mind to work. "What do you need from us?"

Lord Mithrik stood and scooted his chair closer to Devnar's bunk, and Khilam sat next to Devnar and handed him a folded up map from his pocket. Devnar leaned in and listened as the older man listed the atrocities Lady Grenba and Lord Adsel had committed against their people. He forced himself to focus; Melania would be furious at him if he didn't give her a full report when they were reunited.

Now he just had to keep from counting every second until he buried himself inside her again.

Chapter Eleven

Huddled in the corner of the cell, Melania wrapped her arms around her bruised body and stared at the steel wall. She was on a ship headed for the trading base on the moon. Dressed in an ugly bright green jumper, she plucked at the fabric with distaste. This was the color they made the worst criminals wear, those who were considered dead to their families and no longer fit for Kyrimia. Instead of being executed, she was being sent off to what was doubtlessly a life filled with pain and sorrow. She would have almost preferred a quick death if it wasn't for the faint hope that Devnar was still alive.

Everything had happened so quickly, she still tried to figure out how she'd ended up here. Obviously Lady Grenba had set Melania up to take the fall if things went wrong. The only part she couldn't figure out was how in the world Lord Mithrik thought she'd managed to get Devnar onto the planet. She had no smuggling contacts or anything like it. The whole situation didn't make sense.

Denied a trial by the regulators, she'd been whipped in full view of the crowd at the arena before being thrown into an Imperial prison. She had begged for Devnar's life to be spared, but her pleas only met with silence or more beatings. While her physical body hurt, it was nothing compared to the pain of her heart.

She would have gladly confessed to anything, done anything to spare Devnar's life, but it was never given to her as an option. In fact, Lord Mithrik had her gagged soon after she arrived at the prison. The only thing that kept her from losing her mind was the faint sense of Devnar. Somewhere, he was still alive. She didn't get the flashes of emotion she had when he was close, but his spirit was a small, warm ember in her heart.

The door to her cell opened, and she turned her head, blinking against the lights of the hallway. They must have arrived on the moon. Terror at actually being off her planet made a stinging sweat break out over her skin. This was real. This was really happening.

Two guards dressed in dark navy blue leathers sneered at her. "On your feet, traitor."

She pushed herself up and moaned behind her gag as they pulled her to her feet. Since arriving at the jail she had been beaten, often, and her body ached. Never enough to break the skin or harm a bone, but enough so that she had spectacular bruises covering the exposed parts of her body. Barefoot, she followed the men down the hallway to the air lock.

The door opened, and bright light from the trading post made her wince. White walls and floors decorated with pictures of the empress and warnings lined the hallway. More guards waited for them and gave her looks of disgust. "What do you have here?" the female guard with gold braids asked in a brisk voice.

"Lord Mithrik has a new slave for auction." He handed the woman a small disk that she placed into the viewing screen on the table in front of her.

The blonde raised an eyebrow and examined Melania from head to toe. "She's not much to look at."

"She's a breaker." The guard from the ship pushed her forward. "Traitorous bitch smuggled an off-worlder onto Kyrimia."

"Really?" The blonde gaped at her, and her lips thinned into a narrow line. The guard scanned the screen and made a disgusted sound. "Her auction is to be held in one hour. Take her to section 85B and hand her over to a man named Lord Gozil."

Melania's heart sank, and she bit back a moan of despair. Being sold into slavery to an off-worlder was a punishment reserved for only the worst criminals. Horror stories of what happened to slaves who were sold off planet had been the nightmares of her youth. Slavers from all over the galaxy came for the auctions, and the slaves often ended up being sold to whorehouses, where they were used until they died.

The whispered tales of torture and atrocities had her trying to jerk away from her captors and run, though she knew it was useless. Kicking the guard next to her in the kneecap, she bolted toward the door with the mindless panic of a trapped rabbit. Her mind tried to argue about where she was going to run to on the moon, but her dread didn't care.

"Stun her," the blonde said in a bored voice. "I don't want her disturbing the post."

A jolt of pain followed by numbness filled her body, and she fell to the floor. With a grunt, the guard on her right picked her up and slung her over his shoulder. "Don't know who they're going to get to bid on her. Ugly and scrawny. Lord Mithrik will be lucky if he can find a buyer."

Tears of humiliation ran down her face as she bounced against the guard's shoulder. The little warmth inside her she associated with Devnar flared and then went quiet again. Still there but fainter now. The blood rushing to her head pounded in her ears, and she had trouble breathing.

Voices, clanks of metal, and the smell of antiseptics gave her the only hints of the world beyond the guard's back. She had never been to the trader colony before and felt a surge of empathy for Devnar. Was this what he'd felt like when he was captured? He certainly didn't act like it. Wishing she was as strong as he was, she tried to blink away her tears and clear her mind.

A man's silken voice said, "What is that nasty creature you're bringing me? It can't be the breaker Lord Mithrik sent word of. Looks more like an ugly boy with long hair."

The world spun, and her head throbbed as she was set on the floor. She blinked rapidly to try to clear the tears clouding her eyes, and had a watery impression of a short, pale man dressed in brick red robes. Other than his stature, Lord Gozil bore a strong resemblance to Lord Mithrik. Those same dark hazel eyes stared down at her with disgust.

"It is, your lordship." The guards stepped away from her as if she were something foul. Curling, she readied herself for the punch or kick that was surely coming.

"Not much to work with. Her auction is in forty minutes." He clapped his hands and nodded to a lush brunette woman in a soft silver robe. "Belina, take the slave and clean her up as best you can. Put some cellular repair cream on her bruises and wash her. Oh, and her gag stays on. If she tries to resist you, cut her tongue out."

"Yes, your lordship." Belina tugged her to her feet by her hair and wrinkled her nose. Shivering, Melania gave a useless jerk of her head and grimaced as the woman tightened her fist.

Lord Gozil laughed and said to the guards, "Thank you; we'll take good care of the treacherous bitch."

* * *

"Ten ounces of zanthin," a mechanical voice said from the speaker above her head. Standing in the center of a darkened room, unable to make out anything past the glare of the bright lights shining on her, Melania strained to see who was out there bidding on her.

Dressed now in a soft bronze gown slit up the sides to her armpits and held in place by a brown leather belt, she stiffened her shoulders and lifted her chin in defiance. The metal collar around her throat dug into the back of her neck, but she refused to lower her head. If the buyers thought she would be hard to tame, she might be able to avoid being purchased by a whorehouse.

All her years as a breaker served her now as she schooled her body to communicate her will. She would not shrink like a beaten puppy or give any hint of the weakness that attracted predators. The memory of Devnar's ability to dominate a room briefly hurt her heart, but she tried to push the thought away.

Hopefully she would get a new owner, someone unused to slaves and what to do with them. Then all it would take was one opening, and she would escape and find Devnar. With the bond between them, there was nowhere in the universe they could hide him that she couldn't find him. The irony of her thoughts made her lips twist into a bitter smile as the bids continued to rise. Was this how Devnar had felt when he'd been captured? No wonder he'd been so angry with her when they first met. It was truly a miracle that he had moved beyond his hate to love her. She would prove worthy of that gift. She would be brave and strong and be the one to rescue him.

The mechanical voice interrupted her planning, and she rubbed at a healing bruise on her cheek. "Going once, going twice, sold for nineteen ounces of zanthin."

The amount made her raise her eyebrows in shock, but she quickly schooled her face into a bored expression. That was a great amount of money, especially for a slave. Though she had no idea what zanthin was worth to her owner, on her planet that amount would be enough to run her household for years. Too bad whoever bought her had just made the worst deal of their life.

The cellular reconstruction cream itched as it worked on the gash going down her left forearm. Almost healed, the bruises were fading away as well and had gone from black to an ugly yellow. Tension filled her body, and she waited for the door to open and her new owner to claim her.

She began to pace in her little room. The light fabric of the dress fluttered around her, and she clasped her hands together, frowning at the metal cuffs encircling her wrists. Was it only days ago Devnar had wanted her to wear his cuffs? To stretch out beneath him and let him use her body any way he wanted.

Tears threatened to spill over again, and she gave her arm a cruel pinch. No more tears, not where they could see her. To show weakness now would be a mistake. Devnar was waiting for her, relying on her. The only consolation she could give herself was that Lord Mithrik wouldn't give him to Lady Grenba. Even if Devnar was an off-worlder, Lord Mithrik would never let Lady Grenba keep him. Not with the addictive effects of his pheromones.

The door at the end of the room opened, and Belina appeared again. "Your new Master is ready. Hurry up."

Master. Her new owner was male. She followed Belina down the hallway toward where Lord Gozil waited for them. After examining her from head to toe, he nodded at Belina, and she left them alone together.

He twirled a length of red silk between his hands and said, "You've fetched quite a price."

She said nothing, letting her eyes wander around the room as if bored. His chuckle let her know she wasn't fooling anyone. "I suppose it's not that unusual. Once word spread that a real breaker was coming up for auction, we had bidders coming in from all over the galaxy. If I had my way, we would have delayed your sale. But Lord Mithrik wants you away from this planet as soon as possible."

She clenched her hands into fists and fought for control as a brush of anticipation filled her. It pushed past her fear, and she had a moment to ponder it before Lord Gozil snapped her wrist cuffs together. "Your new Master has requested you be blindfolded."

"Why?" The question escaped her lips before she could stop herself. That was a stupid question she already knew the answer to. "Because he owns me, and he wishes it so."

The silk wrapped over her eyes, and she tried to tilt her head to see if she could peek under or around it. Lord Gozil sighed, and she silently cursed him for tying such a good blindfold. The *snick* of a leash fastening to her collar made her stomach clench. She attempted to breathe past her nausea.

"Easy," Lord Gozil murmured.

She had a moment to wonder why he was being so kind with her before a sharp burn pinched her arm. She jerked away and tried to rub her arm with her bound hands. "What did you give me?"

"A mild aphrodisiac and sedative." He gave her a pat on the head like one would give a pet. "You're new Master paid a lot for you. I want you giving him a good ride."

"You bastard." She tried to fight the effects of the sedative as her muscles relaxed against her will.

Warmth flowed through her body, and blood pooled in her groin. The drug traveled through her system, both awakening her and relaxing her. Now she knew why Devnar had hated the aphrodisiacs so much. Being robbed of her ability to choose to feel pleasure was an invasion of the worst kind. Her lower lip trembled as she fought back the despair. No tears. They wouldn't get them from her.

Another man said in a low voice, "I'll take it from here."

She strained against the tug of her leash for a moment before following. Her muscles were slow to respond, and she found her anger slipping away. Contentment flowed through her, followed by a rush of joy. She tried to push past these chemical-induced emotions and focus on her eventual escape.

"Hello, Master," she said in what she hoped was a meek voice.

Nothing, no response to indicate he heard a word she said. Wetting her lips, she took hesitant steps behind him, not trusting him to keep her from running into a wall or hurting herself. They moved through an occupied area of the trade post. Voices and laughter assaulted her heightened sense of hearing, and she stumbled as someone roughly brushed into her.

"Watch where you're going," a woman said in disgust and shoved her roughly.

Unprepared for the shove, she stumbled into a very warm and very big body. He held her and growled out, "Touch her again and you die."

Her body throbbed from her contact with him, and she pushed away. Each rush of desire felt like a betrayal, and his hand brushing down her arm sent tingles over her skin. Without another word, he tugged her leash and led her farther through the post.

"May I ask where we're going, Master?" He took her hand to help her step over a ledge. Silence answered her question, and she gritted her teeth in irritation.

"Your ship is ready, Sir," a cheerful woman's voice said from ahead.

"Thank you," the man pulling her leash said in a low voice, and she shook her head. He sounded familiar, something about the cadence of his tone. If she didn't know better, she would think she knew him. That was probably the drugs muddling her mind. Depending on the aphrodisiac used, she could expect anything from a full mental fuck where they made her believe she was in love with her new Master, to a rush of hormones that would have her humping against anything male that stood still.

Placing a warm hand on her lower back, he led her up a ramp. At the top, they paused, and someone to their left made a low whistle. "Now I see what all the fuss was about."

"Silence," the man barked and jerked her roughly after him. A flare of warmth and anticipation rushed over her, and she stumbled. The strong hand that steadied her lingered on her wrist, stroking the skin with a soft caress. Confusion and anger had her jerking away before she remembered she was supposed to appear harmless.

"Such a brave little thing," he said in a soft voice and ran his thumb along her lower lip.

"Thank you, Master," she said in what she hoped was a simpering tone. If his snort was any indication, she had failed miserably. Damn him, it was so hard to concentrate with the mood swings the drugs were putting her through. First worry, then anger, followed quickly by joy and anticipation. But mainly she felt an overwhelming desire that had her inner thighs wet with her need.

"In you go," he said before pushing her forward with his hands on her bottom.

The door closed behind her, and she turned, reaching forward with her hands. Meeting only the cold metal of the closed door, she reached up to remove her blindfold.

"Don't touch it," another man's voice said.

Chapter Twelve

Melania shivered beneath his voice as if a set of hands were sliding down her hips and cupping her mound. Heat instantly pulsed between her legs, and a rush of liquid warmth wet her inner thighs. Shocked by her visceral response, she pressed back against the closed door in an attempt to cool her body. The drug couldn't work that long; she had to wait it out and hope they made a mistake. As soon as they did, she would kill whoever she had to in order to get to Devnar.

With a *snick*, the bindings holding her wrist together released, and she shook out her hands. The heat of his body touched her before his hands cupped her face. His cheek brushed against hers, and she moaned at the hot rush of lust. "If I had my pick of all the women in the universe, I would still choose you."

His words hit her like a slap, and she stiffened against him. "What did you say?"

Devnar's voice spoke again, his lips brushing her ear. "Is that how you address your Master?"

He made no move to stop her as she pulled the silk scarf from her face, tearing out some strands of hair in her haste. Squinting against the sudden light, she tried to make out the face of the man grinning down at her. A soot black suede shirt accented his broad shoulders and brought out the golden tones in his skin. Dark circles stood beneath his eyes, and the lines around his mouth had deepened.

"Devnar?" Her fingertips trembled as she stroked a hand down his cheek, touching the small scar on his lower lip. "Are you really here, or is this some drug-induced illusion?"

He nipped her finger and sucked it into his mouth. The joy she'd felt earlier blazed through her, and she realized it wasn't drugs she was feeling, but the link of their bond. He released her finger with a smile, and he ran his hands down her body. "I'm really here. Sorry about the drugs, but Lord Mithrik insisted that your role of slave be played out in full."

He swept her into his arms and carried her to the large bed at the back of the room. The floor vibrated beneath her feet as the ship left the port. "For the love of the Gods, tell me what is going on!" She began to cry and shake in his arms as her emotions exploded. He made deep soothing sounds in his throat as he kissed her over and over until she stopped trembling with fear. As his kisses slowed, they changed in tone until her desire reawakened with a vengeance. He seemed to respond to that change in her mood and turned his kiss from gentle to fierce. When his teeth nipped her lower lip, she sighed with pleasure.

He leaned back on the bed with her in his arms and held her so tight she had trouble drawing a breath. "Lord Mithrik knew the moment I landed on your planet that Lady Grenba had smuggled me in, but he didn't know why. He quickly learned who I was and heard rumors of my 'addictive' effects. Curious, he dispatched Khilam to see if it was true while he sent other spies to Lady Grenba's estates to find Bolin and Ikel, my men." His arms eased around her, and she sucked in a deep breath before settling back on his chest. "Lord Mithrik and Khilam learned many things, none of them good. Khilam in particular had to report the bad news that sex with a Jensian is utterly addictive to a Kyrimian."

A new male voice sounded from the doorway. "It wasn't easy convincing Lord Mithrik to not go off and kill every Jensian he could find, starting with Devnar." Melania gave a small scream as Khilam entered the bedroom from the small bathroom and held up his hands as she launched herself at him.

"You bastard!" she screamed and tried to push Devnar's arm off her.

Devnar scrambled forward and grabbed her ankle, dragging her back before she could reach Khilam. "Easy," he whispered, and she relaxed at the scent of his breath. He ran smoothing circles over her arm with his hand. The hormones of his breath fired chemical receptors in her brain that signaled safety and security.

"That's really annoying," she said with a huff and turned to glare at Khilam.

"As I was saying"—Khilam gave her a wide berth and sat on the gray couch across from the bed—"I soon found out that Devnar was extremely addictive." He gave her a wry smile, and she fought a smile as she remembered their time together. "When I reported back to Lord Mithrik what had happened, and after he got over his urge to kill Devnar, we began to suspect Lady Grenba was going to use Devnar to addict the empress—"

"And gain control of her." Devnar lifted her hair off the back of her neck and placed a kiss there that made her shiver. "If Lady Grenba held you, and you commanded me to make love to the empress, I would have had to comply. Without your command, I would be unable to rise to the occasion, and the empress would do anything to get me serviceable again."

Khilam stroked his goatee. "When our spies reached Devnar's men on Lady Grenba's estate, we managed to piece together at least part of her plan. She was going to use Bolin and Ikel as backup to addict the empress in case things fell apart with Devnar. Fortunately we reached Devnar's men before she was able to force them to bond with anyone of her choosing."

Devnar traced the curve of her ear with his finger. "You know how I saw them in the arena? Lord Mithrik entered them on purpose to try and see how both you and Lady Grenba would react to their presence. What he didn't count on was my reaction."

"Or the empress's reaction," Khilam added with a smirk.

Before she could ask what he meant, Devnar stroked his fingers along her collarbone, sending chills through her. "If things had gone Lady Grenba's way, the empress would have been addicted to Bolin and Ikel, and they in turn would have done anything Lady Grenba wanted in order to keep their bond mate safe."

"Leaving Lady Grenba in control of the one thing the empress wanted but could not have." Melania shivered and tried not to imagine what Lady Grenba would have done to convince her and Devnar to go along with her diabolical plan. "So the empress never wanted an off-worlder as a concubine?" She couldn't stop touching Devnar, couldn't stop breathing in a deep lungful of his scent.

Khilam shook his head. "No, she did and does want an off-worlder as her concubine. She thinks that if she is ever going to prove to our people it is time for Kyrimia to rejoin the rest of the galaxy, having an off-worlder as her beloved would go a long way toward changing people's minds." He leaned forward on his elbows. "Lord Mithrik approves of a Jensian as her concubine, especially after seeing how loyal Devnar was with you."

Devnar shifted behind her and pulled her body closer to his. "Over a dozen planets are getting ready to send their best men as candidates. We think Lady Grenba was going to slip me in with the rest and use you to help get me in."

She squirmed away from his hand and turned to face Khilam. "Even if I had managed to get him in, the regulators would have surely noticed. They must be very unhappy about the off-worlders coming here."

"You would think," Khilam said in a dry voice. "We have reason to believe the regulators may have been in on it." He grimaced as she gaped at him. "Powerful forces have been blocking my Lord Mithrik at every turn. We suspect much but can prove little."

"They couldn't figure out if you were in on it or not," Devnar added, and they all rocked as the ship moved into hyperspeed.

"So we set you up." Khilam had the good grace to look embarrassed. "We arranged to have Devnar's men fight at the arena, hoping it would provoke a reaction and give us an excuse to take you into custody while seeing if Lady Grenba would try to rescue you and implicate herself."

"But it worked a little too well. They didn't take into account my battle rage would demand that I rescue my men," Devnar added as he ran his hands down her arms. It was getting increasingly hard to concentrate, especially with his thick erection pressing into her back.

Khilam shifted on the couch and tugged at the edge of his shirt. "With the public scene you caused, Lord Mithrik had to follow through with his threats. Lady Grenba's spies have been watching every move we make, and they tried to outbid Devnar's man, Volun, at the auction."

Devnar rubbed his cheek against her hair. "The bitch has gone into hiding. Lord Mithrik hasn't been able to find her, and we're hoping to follow her agents back to whatever hole she's crawled into. Lord Adsel is somewhere on Jensia, and I promise we are going to do everything we can to find him and make him suffer for his betrayal. I'm sure with me out of the way, he planned to press his case for being the next ruler of my people." His voice dropped to a growl. "With me addicted to Melania, he could control me and make me send a message to my people giving him my support as their leader." His arms tightened, and he buried his face against her neck. "I would do anything to keep you safe."

Leaning back into Devnar's chest, she felt exhaustion wash over her. This still felt like a surreal dream, but she tried to focus on what they were saying. All she wanted to do was wrap Devnar around her like a warm blanket and pretend the last two days had never happened. "Why did Lady Grenba send Devnar to me? I'm one of the last people that would help her against the empress."

"So that he would bond you. She knew from Lord Adsel, one of Devnar's political rivals on Jensia, what kind of woman would attract him. Your natural compassion and kindness would be the sweet trap for his affection. Once you were bonded, she would use you as leverage against him. If he didn't do what she wanted, she would harm you. Lord Adsel told Lady Grenba all about his people and offered her Devnar in exchange for a steady supply of slaves." Khilam's mouth twisted in disgust. "It seems that our races are compatible, that we can breed with one another. Lady Grenba's been smuggling female workers off the planet and sending them to Lord Adsel in exchange for males from your planet."

"That's horrible." She remembered her brief time when she thought she shared their fate, and her throat clenched. "You have to rescue them."

"We're trying, but it's difficult. Lord Mithrik can't send just anyone to help with the search for fear of them becoming addicted to the rebels." Devnar motioned to Khilam and scooted her over so he could sit on the edge of the bed.

Nervous energy moved between them, and she started when Khilam took her hand in his. "There is one thing we found out by accident that can help us."

Devnar's fingers entwined over Khilam's. They both stroked her hand with gentle movements. Watching their hands fold over hers warmed her body and reawakened her desire. Another rush of heat let her know Devnar was as aroused by the sight as she was. Her voice came out husky as she asked, "What's that?"

"Well." Devnar used his other hand to trace the exposed skin of her thigh in light circles. "Khilam shared a bed with one of my men, Uteis, but remained unaffected by his hormones."

"We think my time with you and Devnar keyed my reaction to him. In an effort to better understand Devnar's people, I generously offered myself for experimentation." He grinned at Devnar and gave her hand a squeeze. "While I had a very good time with Uteis, I didn't get the same rush I experienced with you."

"If this is true, then we can pair off your people with mine. Provide them a mate and a hunting partner at the same time." Devnar tensed behind her, and anxiety tinged his voice. "To be honest, we're barely holding off the rebels at it is. Without the help of your people, I don't think we stand much of a chance of finding the women."

After scooting away from Devnar and Khilam, she stood and began to pace. "I can think of a few breakers

I know that would be willing to try. We'll need to contact Pimina. She'll help us arrange for a shelter on Kyrimia that can act as a safe house for those we find." She ran her hands through her hair and turned on her heel as she reached the end of the small room. "I'll also want to set up a safe house on Jensia. Maybe something that mimics the dome structures of Kyrimia. All that open sky has to be a culture shock to our women."

"Melania—"

She waved her hand in a shooing gesture at Devnar and continued, "How big is your planet? What's the environment like? Do you have diagrams or sketches of where the women might be held? What about spies?"

"Melania—"

She stopped and clutched her heart. "What about babies? Oh Gods, they may find a way to get beyond the sterilization. Lady Grenba would have access to the information. Would she have given them the serum?" She chewed on her thumb and resumed pacing. "Those women would never leave their children, but I don't know if the empress would allow them back on the planet. Every child they have will be a baby taken away from someone else. That would lead to deep resentment and I—"

"Concubine, attend!"

Those words cut through her concentration like a laser, and she dropped to her knees with a thud. Khilam snickered, and Devnar elbowed him hard enough to make the other man cough. "Melania, we will take all these things into consideration. But right now, we need your help."

She tried to focus on the here and now, but it was hard knowing about the suffering of all those women. Kneeling helped put her into the right frame of mind to give all her attention to Devnar, so she took a deep breath and met his gaze. "I'm listening."

Khilam exchanged a glance with Devnar. "As we were trying to explain before you went on your tangent"—he ignored her glare and continued—"I need to see if I still respond to Devnar's arousal with the same zeal."

She absently ran her finger under the metal collar around her neck. "I still get the same reaction to his arousal and orgasm. If anything, it's even stronger now."

Devnar patted the bed next to him, and she obliged his silent command. "We don't know if that's because I bonded you or if it's your natural reaction to me."

"With your permission, I would like to be here with you when you and Devnar make love." Khilam glanced at her through his lowered lashes. "I promise I'll sit on the couch and be a good boy."

"Of course." She stood and began to undo the belt around her waist.

"I told you she wouldn't mind," Khilam said with a smirk as Devnar examined her with narrowed eyes.

"Of course I don't mind." She tossed the belt onto the bed and shimmied out of the scrap of bronze silk before crawling onto the bed. Devnar's stunned expression and the rush of his desire lit her body like a flame. "I've had sex in front of others for instruction hundreds of times during my training."

Jaw twitching, Devnar drew her up his body until she draped over his chest. The brush of the soft suede against her nipples had her squirming beneath his touch. "I don't know if I should be happy or jealous."

Khilam reclined on the couch, the evidence of his arousal pressing against the front of his pants. "I know I'm jealous. Melania is a legend among the breakers, for good reason."

His praise brought a blush to her cheeks, and Devnar laughed. "I suggest we make love in front of another man and she doesn't bat a lash. You tell her she's a good breaker, and she blushes like a virgin."

Rough hands stroked down her back, and she nibbled his neck. The taste of his skin brought a soft sigh from her throat, and she arched against him like a cat as he gripped her hips. "I've been going crazy without you," he whispered into her ear. The warmth of his breath paled in comparison to the heat his words brought. The low throb between her legs increased as he licked the shell of her ear. "I'm so sorry I couldn't get you earlier. They locked me in a cell until I agreed to not rescue you and let their plan work. Forgive me."

The kiss she gave him left no doubt how she felt. She tried to push her love through their bond. It must have worked because Devnar shook against her and gave a low groan of pleasure.

A quick jerk at his shirt, and she slid it over his head. For a moment, she could do nothing more than stare at his heavily muscled torso. The soft hair of his body tickled against her skin and gave her a delicious sensation. He stood and swiftly removed his boots and pants. Khilam made a little pained sound from across the room as Devnar bent in front of him. Glancing over his shoulder, Devnar gave him a wicked grin and crawled back onto the bed with her.

All her attention became focused on him as his lips fastened onto her nipple. Strong, harsh sucks had her quickly squirming beneath him. Trying to pull away as he added teeth, and pressing into him as he growled. She couldn't get enough of touching him, the sensation of his skin beneath her fingertips sending sparks of need straight to her swollen pussy.

He sat up and turned her so she faced Khilam, then parted her legs with a firm hand. Another needy sound from Khilam, this time deeper. She leaned back against Devnar's chest, framed by his body as he displayed her for Khilam's hot gaze. The knowledge that Khilam wanted her, that the sight of her body aroused him added to her need. Devnar finally released her nipple and claimed her mouth in a soft kiss. She reached behind her and between his legs to fondle the heavy weight of his sac, stroking the soft skin.

He growled something unintelligible against her lips and parted her labia, spreading her moisture over his fingers and wetting her clit. "I want to watch him fuck you," he whispered against her lips. "Would you like that?" A rush of pure lust rolled off him, and she groaned.

Her hips arched into his fingers, and she shivered in his arms. The lust coming from him increased, and she nodded. It was wonderful to know what he felt, to know what his desires were. No guessing if he meant what he said, no falsehoods between them. She didn't have to worry about jealousy because he knew exactly how she felt about him. She loved him with all her heart. Her trust in him deepened, and his love surged through their bond. "Ask him."

"Khilam, would you like—"

Hands gripped her thighs and spread her wide, throwing her legs over Devnar's thighs. "I thought you'd never ask."

The brush of Khilam's goatee over the swollen folds of her pussy tore a gasp from her. Devnar ate the moans from her lips as surely as Khilam's clever mouth devoured her. Gods, he was talented. Even without Devnar's gift of knowing what she wanted, what she felt, Khilam used his experience to quickly drive her to the edge.

"Stop," Devnar ordered in a rough voice. Pulling back from her grasp, he tweaked her nipple and chuckled as she moaned. "I want you to fuck her."

Khilam didn't even bother to take off his shirt. He pulled down his pants enough to free himself and said, "Open her for me."

Devnar piled some pillows behind him so they sat almost upright. She reached behind her between Devnar's legs and tried to wrap her fist around the width of his hard cock. She gave him an involuntary squeeze as he parted the lips of her pussy and spread her for Khilam's cock. "So wet and pretty," Khilam said with a groan as he pushed his way in.

Devnar stroked her clit, and her body clenched the fat head of Khilam's cock. Slowly Khilam rocked into her, running his cock over different parts of her pussy, judging what she liked by the way she responded to him. Devnar continued to watch, thrusting his cock into her fist in time with Khilam's movements.

She closed her eyes and gave herself over to the sensations. The hot length moving inside her, the thick cock in her hand. And through it all, Devnar's love and need pounding into her soul as surely as Khilam moved in her body.

The bed shifted, and she opened her eyes to find Khilam and Devnar sharing a kiss. Their lips moved and parted in time with Khilam's thrusts, and she gasped. Khilam found her sweet spot and began to work it, stroking faster and harder until she was bucking her hips in a frantic effort to have her release. Devnar's hand unerringly found her clit, and he rubbed it with two of his fingers in a hard circle.

"Fill her with your cum," Devnar said in a deep growl against Khilam's lips.

The rough talk sent her over the edge just as his fingers gave her clit a ruthless pinch. The pleasure of her orgasm tore through her, contracting her muscles in a harsh rhythm that made her scream. Devnar groaned, and his cock throbbed in her fist. Pulling away from her with a jerk, he rubbed the base of Khilam's shaft where it connected with her body.

Head thrown back, an expression of almost pain on his face, Khilam emptied himself into her with a sharp snap of his hips. The sensation of his cock jerking within her body drew out her orgasm, and she ran her hands over Devnar's thigh, seeking his cock, wanting him to join them. He remained out of her reach, but his hungry rumble of need made her body clench as Khilam withdrew.

Khilam's goatee brushed against her cheek as he collapsed next to her and ran his hands over her breasts. Devnar moved from behind her back, and her head rested against the bed next to Khilam's. They both leaned up to watch Devnar settle between her thighs. One delicate lick on her oversensitive flesh had her clutching the sheets. She and Khilam exchanged a stunned glance as Devnar's lust rode over them.

The stiff length of his tongue thrust into her channel, licking out Khilam's cum. So good. His tongue moved in broad and greedy strokes as he groaned and rubbed his face against her thigh. "You have no idea how good you taste. Your passion and his, mixed together. You taste like the essence of life." He sucked on her clit and held her hips down as she tried to scramble away from him. It was too much too soon after her orgasm, but he was relentless. Khilam bit and sucked on her neck, gentle touches that confused her body until too much became just right. Helpless between them, she could only feel.

The brush of Khilam's lips traveled down to her breast, and he circled the aching tip with his lips. She moaned in protest as Devnar pulled away. A few more licks and she would have been over the edge again. "Hold her hands over her head," Devnar said and positioned himself between her thighs.

The feeling of Khilam's strong hands holding her down allowed her to sink deeper into her body. Thought became unimportant as she surrendered herself completely to Devnar. The nudge of his cock at her slick entrance had her eyelids closing without conscious thought. In darkness, she rode the flow of emotions through their bond as surely as she rode his cock.

There was no give in Khilam's grip as she struggled against the power of Devnar's thrusts. He pounded into her body, ripping sensations from her with no mercy. His need for her pushed against her heart, and she opened her emotions to him. Love poured into her soul, filling her until she thought it would burst. He stiffened against her, and his orgasm crashed into her, triggering her own until she was caught in an endless loop. Above her, Khilam let out a strangled groan, and his hands convulsed on her wrists. One crest would wash through her quickly, followed by another until the world turned white.

Devnar barely rolled to his side as he fell onto her, both of them shivering and twitching with the aftershocks of their orgasm. Holding her close, he pulled Khilam down to her other side until they spooned her. Eyes closed, she luxuriated in the sensation of rough and smooth hands stroking her. Devnar's unique scent filled her mind and body until she could feel the beat of his heart moving her blood.

Behind her, Khilam let out a breathless chuckle and rubbed his face into her long hair. "Well, I think we can safely say I still react to Devnar the same."

She made a sleepy sound of agreement and sighed as Devnar placed gentle kisses on her forehead. The security and strength of his love filled a void in her soul so completely she felt like she had been reborn. No more living one day to the next with only the purpose of existing. She had a reason and a man to live for that went beyond all her wildest dreams.

"I almost forgot." Khilam pulled away. She complained about missing his warmth and watched the firm muscles of his backside work as he crossed the room to dig through his discarded clothes. He quickly returned, and she snuggled between them as Devnar pulled Khilam against her back.

"What's that?" Devnar asked, and his chest moved against her face as he leaned back.

She turned and examined the small golden glass vial Khilam held. He stroked her hair back from her face and placed a kiss on her temple. "A gift and an apology from the empress. She is sorry for all the pain that you went through and appreciates your loyalty to her."

"It can't be…" She reached up and touched the vial with a trembling fingertip.

"It is."

"Is what?" Devnar let her take the vial from Khilam, and his contentment was replaced with unease.

"A baby," she whispered and clutched the vial to her chest.

"Or babies," Khilam said with obvious pleasure in his voice. "Being that you will be living on Jensia with Prince Devnar, the empress has given you leave to have as many children as you wish with him. She wants to heal the breach between our people that Lady Grenba and Lord Adsel's greed caused."

Pride and joy to rival her own rushed through her as Devnar processed the information. "I love you."

She cupped his face and traced the crooked line of his nose and the scar on his lower lip. "I love you too."

They shared a gentle kiss as Khilam made a happy sound behind her. Cradled in their arms, she let her mind fill with dreams of a future where she would never be alone again.

Ann Mayburn

Ann is Queen of the Castle to her wonderful husband and three sons in the mountains of West Virginia. In her past lives she's been an import broker, a communications specialist, a US Navy civilian contractor, a bartender/waitress, and an actor at the Michigan Renaissance Festival. She also spent a summer touring with the Grateful Dead-though she will deny to her children that it ever happened.

From a young age she's been fascinated by myths and fairytales, and the romance that often was the center of the story. As Ann grew older and her hormones kicked in, she discovered trashy romance novels. Great at first, but she soon grew tired of the endless stories with a big, wonderful, emotional buildup to really short and crappy sex. Never a big fan of purple prose (throbbing spears of fleshy pleasure and wet honey pots make her giggle), she sought out books that gave the sex scenes in the story just as much detail and plot as everything else without using cringe worthy euphemisms. This led her to the wonderful world of erotic romance, and she's never looked back.

Now Ann spends her days trying to tune out cartoons playing in the background to get into her 'sexy space' and has learned to type one handed while soothing a cranky baby.

Main Web site: http://www.annmayburn.com

Facebook: http://www.facebook.com/people/Ann-Mayburn/100001759870653

Follow her on Twitter: @AnnMayburn

Loose Id® Titles by Ann Mayburn

*Available in digital format at http://www.loose-id.com
or your favorite online retailer*

The Breaker's Concubine

* * * *

The VIRTUAL SEDUCTION Series
*Sodom and Detroit
Sodom and the Phoenix*

The Breaker's Concubine *is also available in print*

CPSIA information can be obtained at www.ICGtesting.com
Printed in the USA
LVOW08s0400110114

368942LV00005B/973/P